SHEPHERD
OF THE
BLACK SHEEP

KRISTOPHER TRIANA

ISBN 978-1-940250-31-1

Artwork by Jeff West

Printed in the United States of America

First Edition

Visit us online at
www.bloodboundbooks.net

For Danielle
Because you'll always be my little sister

Save your people and bless your inheritance;
be their shepherd also, and carry them forever.

~ **Psalm 28:9**

PROLOGUE

There were two little girls in the woods.

They stood in their boots, ankle-deep in the snow, jackets open to the winter breeze that blew long hair about their shoulders. Gentle flurries had fallen through the dead fingers of the branches above them, dusting their wool caps and making the little balls on top look like snow globes.

At ten and a half, Alice was the younger of the two by a few months—a pretty blonde with a splash of freckles across her nose and cheeks, lips in need of ChapStick. In her hands was a spiral notebook filled with notes and stories pertaining to Sopheria, the magical fairyland she and her best friend Paige had created together. Paige stood across from Alice with her own notebook in hand. It contained some of their other stories and notes, including illustrations she'd done in multicolored pen.

Paige was quiet and passive. There was a hushed sadness behind her eyes, reflecting the amount of hardship she'd seen for such a young girl, hardship Alice couldn't understand. Paige's sad brown eyes matched her hair, which was so dark it appeared black in the gray light of the afternoon, blacker than even her mother's had been when she was alive.

Paige would be eleven in March, and was also eleven inches taller than her friend, but her size and seniority didn't stop Alice from being the bossy one.

"Let me see," Alice said, taking Paige's notebook.

She flipped to the middle of the book where they'd left off the day before. They'd only had a few hours yesterday after school, but now it was Saturday, and they could spend most of the day together. Even in the chill of December they always worked together on their Sopheria stories and characters at the same spot in the woods. They would make notes while they were apart, but all of the final decisions had to be made here in their private cove, together. Though they never spoke of it, both girls felt that the magic of their fantasyland could be harmed, perhaps even broken, by interference from the outside world—especially grownups.

"I think Sir Rowan should ask Princess Katandra for her hand in marriage," Alice said. "He's beaten the great beast Og. He is the bravest knight in all of Sopheria."

Paige nodded. "Yeah. But Slagon is coming."

"Once he leads the Knights of Rose to victory over The Dark Ones, he will return home to take Katandra's hand, and all of Sopheria will celebrate!"

Faint snow began to fall about them. Then there was a rustling sound, and when Alice looked up her smile faded. The wind grew fiercer, colder, and there was a sudden flash of steel catching the muted sunlight just before the two girls started screaming, and only one was able to run away.

PART ONE

BLESS THE BEASTS AND CHILDREN

CHAPTER ONE

THREE DAYS EARLIER

From atop his horse, Tom Hargrave looked past the livestock pens and out into the open pastures that wound down the snowy slope. Tapping the Appaloosa, his spurs jangled like sleigh bells, and the horse moved on down the path that was partly camouflaged by the fresh dusting of snow. The horse's coat matched the land—white with spots of brown, accompanied by the striped hooves, mottled muzzle and the white sclera in the eyes that made it a true Appaloosa. The chill of daybreak was deep and wet. Mist rose from the horse's nostrils.

Tom gathered the reins. "Come on now, girl."

Old Essie was his favorite horse on the ranch, but at twenty she was getting on in years, and Tom had found that she'd gotten fussier in that time. He got her trotting down to the automatic water basin where he'd lined up the heated buckets. Now that winter was making its intentions clear, Tom could see he'd have to do some shoveling if they were going to be accessible. In a way he'd always liked the snow because it covered the smell of the cow turds, but as he'd gotten older the cold had grown meaner, harder on his bones. He still did much of his own work on the ranch, digging postholes and flanking cattle. He was already looking forward to springtime when mother nature would take a little pity on his hands, back and toes. But it wasn't even Christmas yet. He had a long way to go and so did his livestock.

Christmas, he thought. *What the hell am I gonna do without Betty or Dawn?*

He'd never been good at buying gifts. He'd always struggled picking presents for Betty when she was still alive, and after she died it made it all the harder for him to pick them out for their daughter. Dawn was grown by then, but somehow that just made it more difficult. And if he hadn't been good at picking out gifts for his daughter, somehow he doubted he'd do much better with his granddaughter, Paige. How could he make their first Christmas together special?

"I'm an old man," he said to the horse. "I don't know what these kids today want. Seems like all they like is phones." He often spoke to himself, but when he directed it at the animals it didn't make him feel like he was getting soft in the skull. "Ain't giving no cell phone to no ten-year-old girl. You can believe that, Essie." The horse snorted as if in reply and Tom cracked a grin. "Damn Christmas is a pain, ain't it, girl? But I guess there are worse things."

He could think of plenty worse things. The approaching holiday weighed down on him like wet sandbags, but beneath that was the anxiety of the forthcoming years of holidays and other milestones kids go through. Paige had been with him for eleven months now, but this would be her first Christmas here on the ranch with Tom, and also the first Christmas without her parents. She had never been a very talkative child, and little had changed after the accident. She was damaged from it, surely, still grieving. He understood that. His own grief had gone from a sharp, debilitating misery to a dull ache that stalked him like a vulture. Tom never thought he'd be burying his own child. But while he was trying his damnedest to connect with Paige, the girl seemed to drift more and more away.

Paige seemed even quieter than normal, more prone to playing in her room alone instead of pestering him or blasting the TV. Most of the time she was writing or drawing pretty pictures—fairies, unicorns, knights in shining armor. He liked to encourage that, but at the same time he felt like she was too withdrawn. He worried this isolation might stunt her social skills. It made him blame himself for not having any answers when it came to lifting her out of that pit of sadness he knew too well. He'd writhed in it years ago when Betty had been diagnosed with blood cancer, and could have suffocated in it when Dawn and her husband died in that wreck, had it not been for his responsibility to take care of Paige. He stifled his grief for the kid's sake and tried to focus on the fact that he was her guardian now, no matter how big of a surprise that had been.

He was happy to care for Paige. She was his kin and he loved her. But being a sixty-five-year-old widower didn't make him the most likely caregiver for such a young girl.

A grandson would have been easier, he thought. Tom understood what came with boys—the sports and the roughhousing, the bravado of the male ego. He'd been a boxer in his younger days and understood the competitive drive that came with testosterone. But that knowledge hadn't done much good when raising his own son. He hadn't raised Scott any better than he had his daughter, so maybe understanding one sex better than another didn't amount to much.

At the far end of the fence, Tom looked out at the valley that stretched toward the thick expanse of woods. The trees were slouched, burdened by snow, and he couldn't see or hear any birds. In the distance, a branch must have snapped under the weight of the snow, and in the thick silence its crack was as loud as a gunshot. It made him flinch and Essie riled beneath him, spooked. He patted her.

"Easy, easy."

Looking over the ranch, he let out a long exhale. This was his land, his home, a place that had absorbed so much of his love and sweat. Somehow it had transformed into something he'd never intended it to be, a cursed dirt haunted by the echo of a family lost, a family he felt he'd failed. This ageless land was tainted now, a valley where dreams had shattered like glass and only the memories that stung seemed to stick. But it was his land and all he knew: these hills, these cattle, these sheep and the cold, hard earth itself.

He hoped he could continue to learn from it and not let it swallow him like that pit of sadness. He could also learn from his granddaughter, as long as he remembered to listen. She wasn't bitter toward him or distant like his son Scott had become, and she wasn't lost forever the way her poor mama was. Paige was a clean slate. Only now was she getting to know him. He wanted to make the right impression, and not just with simple Christmas gifts.

Having Paige isn't a burden, he thought. *It's a second chance.*

CHAPTER TWO

Tom glanced at his granddaughter as she stretched out on the floor. She lay on her belly, propped up on her elbows as she worked on the puzzle that was splayed out on a plastic play mat. It was one of the thousand-piece ones Betty had loved. A picture of Van Gogh's almond branches was on it. Paige was good at the puzzles, and when she did them she displayed a quiet contemplation that was beyond her years. She was well past dolls now and demanded more of a challenge from toys, such as friendship bracelet kits and the old electronic *Simon* game she'd found out in the shed, which had been Scott's once upon a time.

It was Wednesday night and while she had homework he figured she still had a few hours to get it done. He had let her play in the woods with Alice until the sun started to go down, and Paige had pouted because it got dark so early this time of year, but she had obeyed him, so he wasn't about to get on her case about math and social studies just yet.

He could see her from the kitchen. He was making himself a steak and would have liked Paige to try out one of these sirloins from the most recent slaughter, but she was young and finicky, so he was making her a chicken cutlet, also from the ranch. Unlike the cattle, which he sent off for processing, he killed and defeathered his own chickens just like his mother had taught him to when he was a boy. Paige liked peas, so that was her side dish, with a small bowl of applesauce for desert.

Jep, his yellow lab, sat by his side, watching the food intently, obedient enough to not touch it or jump up.

Tom tossed him a scrap. "There you go, boy."

Jep was more than a pet. He was a herding dog. When Tom had to move the cattle Jep did a good deal of the work. He'd brought him in as a free-to-a-good-home puppy and trained him well so he could be a replacement for Red, who had gotten on in years and died last spring to be buried in the backyard with the other dogs he'd loved. Tom's life had been filled with so much death lately, a series of blows that were almost too many to absorb.

He called to Paige. "You and Alice have fun today?"

"Yeah."

Sometimes getting more out of her than one-word answers was like running in the sand. Other times he couldn't get a clear answer out of her at all.

"What'd y'all get into?"

"Huh?"

"What was y'all doin?"

"Nothing."

"Nothin? Well, that don't sound like much fun. When I was your age I always liked to have *fun*. And while I ain't got much energy for it these days I still appreciate it when it comes my way."

He failed to get a laugh out of her. She kept trying to fit a piece into the puzzle that didn't seem to want to go anywhere.

"We just played," she said, still looking at the puzzle. "You know."

He liked that the girls played in the woods. It was good for them, and not enough kids did that these days. He'd seen on the news that a couple of parents had gotten in trouble with the law just for letting their kids walk to and from the park alone. The law said it was neglect. Tom didn't know what to make of that. It seemed like madness.

"Dinner's just about ready, darlin. How bout you come in and set the table. Feed Jep too."

Paige got up and went into the kitchen. By the time the food was ready the table was set, Jep was chomping kibble, and Paige had poured herself a glass of milk and gotten Tom a seltzer from the fridge. It's what he drank these days in place of beer. When they started eating he tried again to get a conversation going.

"How was school today?"

"Good."

"Care to elaborate?"

She shrugged, and he put his fork down.

"Somethin wrong, darlin?"

"No." Her eyes stayed on the food she was playing with but not eating.

"If there is, you know you can talk to me, dontcha?"

"Yeah."

There was a silent moment.

"You know, I was thinkin about gifts today, what with Christmas comin and all. Anythin you're hopin Santa will bring ya?"

Her voice was low. "There's no Santa Claus. That's kids' stuff."

"Well, I know. Figure I was just bein cute there. Sorry."

"That's okay."

He was happy to see her take a spoonful of peas.

"So? Anythin special you want? You gotta help your old granddad out. He's not so good at guessin."

Another shrug. "I'm not sure. I'll think about it."

He almost began to tell her some of the things her mother had enjoyed at her age but decided against it. Something told him it was better not to bring up her parents right now. Their absence this year was bound to make Christmas hard on her. It was hard on Tom too. Being depressed during the holidays was common, but not for a ten-year-old. It went against nature—just like losing both your parents before you'd even entered junior high.

Paige slipped some food under the table. It was against the rules, but Tom let it slide because he liked seeing her form any kind of bond with the dog. Sometimes she seemed isolated even from the animals. She helped him around the ranch and took good care of the chickens, but she never seemed excited to be around them the way most kids were.

She glanced up at him and smiled. It was a little forced, but he appreciated it anyway. He smiled back at her and noticed that she looked past him now, over his shoulder and out the front window. He turned and looked, seeing that it was snowing again. Fat flakes whizzed past the glass like summer moths, adding to yesterday's two feet of snow that still hadn't melted.

"How bout a new sled?" he asked. "That old plastic one is fallin apart. Maybe you could use one of the old fashion steel and wood ones. They're sturdier."

"Okay."

She seemed to perk up at the idea and he made a mental note.

"Any other games ya like?"

She thought for a moment. "Mom and I used to play the game of hands. Do you know that one?"

He did. He'd forgotten all about it, but it came flashing back into his mind, the nostalgia warm and rust-colored.

"Know it?" he said. "I invented it."

"Really?"

"Sure, didn't your mama tell ya that?"

"I can't remember. She taught it to me when I was little. I can't remember ever *not* knowing it."

It was a simple game really. He'd played it with his kids, especially when they were out somewhere and getting restless. It had started with Scott, who loved the game so much that he helped create new signs for it. The original line-up of signs was easy to understand. Tom would take one of his kids' hands and would pump or shake them, or he would use one to three fingers and put them in their palm. Each of these was a code, like a form of sign language. Of course, this wasn't actual sign language—Tom had just made the signals up—but it worked as a private language all the same. One pump of the hand meant the number one, and so on up to ten. One finger in the palm meant yes, two meant no, three meant maybe. There were also signs for add, subtract and multiply. He would use these to play little math games with them, and sometimes a quiet form of Twenty Questions. As Scott grew older he added signs for colors, animals, and elements. Dawn loved the game as well, and while Tom's wife knew about it she never learned the codes or tried to wedge herself into the special, secret little game her husband shared with their children.

It touched him to know Dawn had passed the game down to Paige.

He took his granddaughter's hand and pumped it with two plus two.

Her hand answered four and they both smiled. He upped the challenge, giving her six times five, and she gave him thirty by giving him ten pumps, a multiply signal, and then three more pumps. She took a turn then, giving him yellow plus blue. He gave her green and was surprised at how many of the codes he still remembered. It came back to him like a dream suddenly recalled during a morning shower.

They played like that for some time, grinning in silence, their eyes talking for them.

He'd already fed all the livestock, which he had to do now that the fields were frozen, so after dinner he went to his favorite chair and turned on ESPN to watch a welterweight boxing match. Paige cleaned up in the kitchen, part of her regular chores, then brought her schoolbooks out to the table to start on her homework. He appreciated that Paige did these things on her own. It was another quality that set her apart from other kids her age.

She's a good kid, he thought. She was quiet and distant sometimes, a black sheep in her way, but that didn't make her bad. Just different.

The fight was a real brawl, neither boxer dancing around the ring. When he'd been a fighter in his younger days, Tom had always tried to mirror Muhammad Ali by using the rope-a-dope, feigning being trapped in a corner so his opponent would tire himself out with ineffective punches. A lot of these modern fighters lacked such creativity in the ring and Tom felt the sport suffered for it. He still watched the match, but his mind wandered to the winter maintenance that lay ahead of him. There was still more wood to chop and perimeter fence checks to do. Paige could help him with some of it, but he'd have to hire help for the season, maybe get some of the local teens to do some of the backbreaking stuff he had trouble handling these days. If he talked to Dale he could spread the word around the youth center.

"Grandpa," Paige called from the kitchen.

"Yes, darlin?"

"There's a man outside."

Tom turned in his chair. "What's that?"

"There's a man. He's out front of the house."

≻⚊

Tom went to the window. Jep shadowed him and started barking, sensing the stranger wandering around their front yard. The ranch was on the outskirts of town, surrounded by the dense woods of Coyote Valley and its rolling, open prairie. There were other ranches and farmhouses out on this stretch, and a small suburb on the other side of the thicket, but Tom's closest neighbor was Fred Hollister and he lived almost a quarter mile down the road.

This wasn't Fred.

Hollister was an overweight pecan farmer. The man stumbling through the yard was slim and taller than Fred, dressed in a black trench coat and ski cap. He seemed to be struggling to stay on his feet, his rain boots plunging in and out of the snow. He wasn't heading for the front door. He seemed to be walking toward the side of the house.

"What's he doing out there?" Paige asked.

Tom went to the coat rack and put on his winter jacket and Stetson. "That's what I plan to find out. You stay in here with Jep and keep away from the windows."

"How come?"

"Just do like I tell ya."

He opened the hall closet, reached in for the double barrel Browning, made sure it was loaded and snapped it back together. He slung it over his shoulder the way he'd been taught to in the army. Betty would have said he was being paranoid. Maybe he was, but it

8

was wise to be ready to protect yourself, especially when you lived this far from town. The man in the yard was on Tom's property and didn't appear to be making a delivery or house call. He was a stranger and might not be alone.

Unlatching the door, Tom put his hand on his granddaughter's shoulder. "Lock the door behind me. And don't you open it for anybody but me, okay? Make sure it's me before you open it."

Her eyes darted. "Grandpa, I'm scared."

"Don't worry. We're just bein careful."

A gust of frigid air accosted Tom as he stepped outside. The stranger continued to stagger, seeming not to notice him. Tom heard the door bolt behind him and he glanced at the road, looking for a stuck car. He didn't see one. The man was about to round the corner of the house when Tom called out to him.

"Hello there."

When the man spun around, Tom swung the shotgun off his shoulder but kept it low, not aimed, neutral. The man was unarmed but he also didn't put his hands up at the sight of the gun. Between the snow and the distance Tom could barely make out his face. It was pink and pulpy, a wad of hamburger.

"You wanna tell me what you're doin on my land?"

The man looked around, as if realizing where he was for the first time. He took a few slow steps, coming toward Tom as he stood his ground. There was some angry swelling under the stranger's right eye, as if he'd been in a fight. Now the man's hands went up in a passive manner, and as he got closer Tom saw that his face was bright but chalky, probably frostbitten. He was young, but also haggard, the lines in his face telling of nights spent inside a bottle, maybe even curled up with a needle or pipe. About a week's worth of stubble made a nest of his face and his yellowed teeth chattered like chains when he spoke.

"It's cold out."

"Sure is," Tom said, "but that don't answer my question."

"Out walkin. Lost track of time, maybe."

"Where'd you come from?"

"Boston."

This was no surprise. The man had a thick New England accent. Tom had one too when it came to certain words, but with his parents being from Oklahoma he maintained a slight southern twang that made it hard for people to guess where he was from.

"You're a long way from home, son," he said. "This here is Old

Middlebury. Coyote Valley to be exact."

The man gazed up into the whitewashed sky, as if entranced by the snow that tumbled down upon them, growing heavier, denser. He seemed to be drifting away, likely high on something.

Tom's brow furled. "You know you're in Vermont, right?"

The man nodded halfheartedly.

"You on the road?"

"Yeah."

"No car?"

He shook his head.

"So you're a drifter then?"

"On the road, yeah."

A gentle wind whistled, sending horizontal flakes between them.

"What's your name, son?"

The man hesitated. "Jason."

"Well listen up, Jason. Town is east of here. This is private property and I don't like nobody snoopin around, understand?"

"Okay."

"You're right, it is cold out here. I can call my friend, Sheriff Dale Rogers. He can arrange a ride for you so you won't lose a toe in this weather. But you'll have to wait down by the mailbox."

The stranger looked away. "No, no. That's okay. I'll just go."

"Go and stay gone. If I catch you on this ranch again you'll have me and my dog to reckon with, and neither of us are gonna be very friendly."

Jason was already trudging toward what could still be seen of the gravel driveway. Tom watched, ready to raise the barrel at any sudden movements, and smiled when he heard Jep bark from inside the house, making a threat of his own. Jason walked faster once he was out of the heavy snow, and the night and whirling snowflakes swallowed him up as he wandered back toward the state road. Tom watched him until he was nothing more than a black dot heading west, away from town instead of toward it. Once he was out of sight, Tom headed back inside to call Dale.

CHAPTER THREE

"These drifters show up from time to time." Dale sipped his coffee. "Though usually not this far from town. He must've really been hopped up to be wandering around in this kinda cold."

Tom shifted in his seat, leaning in. "Maybe we should go back out and look for him. Couldn't have gotten far."

"I'm tellin you, Tom, I drove up and down the road and didn't see anythin but snow. I've got two of my deputies patrollin and checkin in on your neighbors. That's all we can do."

"I didn't like the way he was walkin around the house."

"I don't blame you. He may have been up to no good, but he may have just been high, like you said. He seem paranoid?"

Tom shook his head. "He seemed like he was in a trance or somethin. Like he was on acid, I guess."

Dale rolled his eyes. "Saw enough of that shit in the A Shau Valley."

"The boys used it in Da Nang too."

The two men had grown up together, but while Dale had chosen to serve, Tom had been drafted. He spent a year and a half over there, and saw a little action, which had been more than enough. But Dale stayed in Vietnam for three years, then Cambodia for another eight months before being honorably discharged and receiving a Purple Heart. Tom suspected Dale had seen far more action than he had, but it was something they never spoke about.

Dale ran a hand through his russet hair. "Well, it sounds like we've got a transient space cadet. Potential burglar. But he might've just been lookin for someplace warm to sleep. Might've been headin for your barn."

Jep came over to the table and nuzzled up to Dale. The sheriff scratched him behind the ear.

Tom put his elbows on the table. "What gets me is he didn't seem too scared when I held up the Browning. Didn't faze him at all."

"Well, they've got guns down in Boston too."

Tom glowered. "I don't wanna see that boy around here again."

"You know you've got every right to protect yourself. But you see him, don't go out after him, just call me right away. Maybe we can snatch him up before he disappears again." Dale slurped down the last of his coffee.

"Get you another?"

Dale rose from his seat. "Thanks, but I've got paperwork to do if I'm ever gonna finish up for the night."

"How the hell does a town with hardly ten people in it keep you so busy?"

"Ask the taxpayers when it comes time to vote on better fundin for the department."

They chuckled and Tom stood to show him out. As they moved through the living room, Paige glanced up from her book and waved to the sheriff.

"Goodnight, Mr. Rogers."

"Goodnight, darlin. And if I don't see you before Christmas, you have a merry one, ya hear?"

"Merry Christmas."

At the door, Dale patted Tom on the shoulder. "She seems to be doin good these days."

"I think so," he said, though it wasn't always true.

"Welp, this time of year gets kids happy. Try and enjoy it, old man. We both know how damn fast they grow up."

CHAPTER FOUR

As usual in the winter months, Tom waited with Paige for the school bus the next morning. There were only three other kids at the stop— the Godfrey boys and Alice MacDougall, Paige's best friend who lived on the other side of the hill. Alice's mother let her join them in Tom's truck and drove off. The Godfrey boys stayed warm in their mother's station wagon. Alice was certainly plenty warm, dressed in so many layers that Tom thought she looked like the Stay Puft Marshmallow Man.

He hadn't heard anything from Dale about the drifter. There was probably nothing to be heard, which was bittersweet. It was a relief to know this Jason character hadn't broken into anyone's house or done something worse, and it seemed like he may have moved on. But Tom would prefer Jason be picked up so he could be sure he wasn't anything to be concerned about. Last night, after Dale had left, Tom kicked himself for letting Jason wander off. He should have called Dale before going out there and kept the stranger around until the sheriff arrived.

Beside Tom, the two girls were looking at a magazine and talking about the clothes in it, which reminded him that Paige would be a teen before he could blink, and then he'd really be tested.

"I like the pink sweater best," Paige said.

Alice pursed her lips. "No way. Pink is for babies."

"Well, I like it."

"It's an okay sweater, but it would have been better in purple."

Tom couldn't help but notice that Alice was dressed in purple snow pants and a purple sweater. The kid knew what she liked.

The snow let up by daybreak, but it had hammered through the night in a white wall. One either side of the road the plows had made dunes that were four feet tall, peppered with twigs and clumps of dirt. There would be a lot of work to do on the ranch, and a lot of feeding. After he'd seen the girls off to school he was going to head into town, get some supplies from Ed's, and see about hiring a few helpers. His land wasn't that big for a ranch, and he had a limited amount of cattle—which he processed and sold to the grass-fed markets and the local shops downtown—so two or three ranch hands would be enough.

The bus pulled in with a screech and the fat Godfrey boys bumbled their way out of the station wagon like a pair of puppies sliding on a hardwood floor. Tom reached over the girls and opened the door to the truck. Alice hopped down, followed close behind by Paige. The two of them were as tight as sisters, tighter even because they never fought, and Tom was grateful that Alice was part of Paige's life. It had helped her start to think of Middlebury as home. The town was a long way from Amherst, Massachusetts, where she'd been born, raised and then yanked out of after the shock of her parents' sudden death. Maybe that distance would prove to be a good thing, a divider between what she'd lost and what lie ahead.

"Y'all be good now," he told them.

"Bye," they said in unison, and then they were off, kicking up tufts of packed snow as they ran to the bus.

Tom turned the old F150 around and headed toward town, listening to the country station until he could no longer stand the new pop stuff. He grimaced at the pandering of it, missing the real deals like Waylon, Merle and Cash, the songs he'd grown up on. He never heard them on the radio anymore, just this hokey stadium horseshit. It seemed that with each passing year the world around him became harder for him to understand.

Sometimes it seemed like America's authenticity had been replaced by shiny plastic and easily-replaced gizmos, all of it cheap and uninspired, soulless and without heart. There was a hollowness to this new culture, built as a means to get a quick buck by providing the masses with a moment of mindless distraction. None of it was enough to make a lasting impression, and it kept him out of movie theaters and confused him when he watched TV. It made Tom wince when he saw people walking around with their faces buried in their phones, texting instead of calling, all of them junkies hooked on the internet. He knew it was easy to romanticize the past, and how well nostalgia could take the rough edges off of things, but this was more than him just getting older and growing bitter toward the younger generations. He didn't necessarily believe *everything* was better in the old days, but he sure didn't like the way things were now.

As he got into town he headed toward The Blue Streak Diner and found a spot in the street he could just barely fit the truck in due to the snow piles. Getting out, he pulled his coat tight against the mean December wind, jogged into the diner and grabbed a stool at the counter. It was early on a weekday but there were still ten people inside. Russ was refilling Maurice Johnson's mug while they talked about the high school football team. When he spotted Tom he nodded, but it was Hannah Green who approached first. She was a heavyset woman of forty, with a dimpled chin and a genuine smile that never left her cheeks. Two pencils were keeping her hair up in a bun the size of a cinnamon roll.

"Mornin, Tom. How you doin today, darlin?"

"Tryin to stay warm, lookin to get fat and happy."

"Well, we're always happy to see ya. How them bossies doin? You gonna have some more cuts for us soon?"

"Sure, just hope you don't mind them bein frozen. Don't think the herd's gonna thaw for four months with this snow we've been gettin."

She groaned. "Ain't that the truth. Took my Ed two freakin hours to shovel out the walk and driveway. Wish he'd let me help him. He's gonna give himself a heart attack one of these days."

Her husband was even bigger than she was, a working-class hero type who ran the feed store on Maple Avenue.

"I'll be seein him shortly," Tom said. "Think he knows of anyone lookin for work?"

"Oh, I don't know. We've been married so long that when he gets to talkin business I just tune him out."

Tom laughed at her honesty.

"Want the usual, I'm guessin?"

He winked. "Yes, ma'am."

The Blue Streak's hash brown plate couldn't be topped, and he always ordered them with chicken and waffles. In Middlebury, Vermont, eating a breakfast without maple syrup was like singing in an elevator—you could do it, but it was generally frowned upon. She went to put the order in and wait on the other customers, and Russ strolled over to say good morning.

"Catch the fight last night?" he asked.

Russel Redburn was a svelte man, five years older than Tom, with a rosy complexion and silvery hair that was always plastered to his scalp with pomade. He'd long owned the diner and continued to work there each day, more for the social activity than anything else.

Tom nodded. "Yeah, I saw some of it."

"It was pretty good. More brawling than boxing. Weird for a welterweight bout, but I like when they duke it out. Course I was never no golden gloves champ like you, so I don't know as well as you would, but still, I'd expect more technique, you know?"

"Yeah, sure seemed that way from the bit I caught. Don't rightly know what's happened to the sport. In boxing, skill is more important than muscle. Seems there's no real contenders anymore."

Russ crossed his arms. "I blame Money Mayweather. And those Klitchko brothers pickin and choosin who they wanna fight. Now we got these bozos comin into the ring wearin Halloween masks for Christ's sake, like it's WrestleMania instead of the sport of kings. I tell ya, we need another Sugar Ray, a real people's champion."

"Yeah, that'd be nice."

Russ paused. "Heard about your visitor last night. Scary stuff there, Tom."

He blinked. "Oh... yeah. That."

"Cooper was in here earlier. Said Dale sent him out on the call to look for the guy but he and the boys couldn't find him. Said he was a real creeper."

"A creeper?"

"You know, snoopin around houses. Must be a burglar, or one of them peepin Toms." He chortled. "No offense. Not all *Toms* are peepers."

"Don't be so sure."

He went along with the levity, but what Russ said startled him. He hadn't even considered the drifter might be some sort of pervert. It made Tom feel cold in spite of the heat blasting down from the vents.

What if he'd seen Paige and followed her home?

Russ leaned on the counter. "Cooper said you scared him off with a shotgun."

"Ayuh."

"Good to see a man stand his ground. Too many sissies out there today think a man shouldn't have a gun in his own home. Think they're not needed. I'd like to see how they feel when some creeper comes around their house like that."

"Well, I hope this guy just headed on out of town. I think he was a drifter. So does Dale."

"Even us small towns can't stay clean of em these days. Too many people outta work. Damn economy's shot to hell."

Tom sat up straight and slapped his hands on the counter. "Well I'm lookin to boost the job market, Russ. I needed some strong young dudes to help me around the ranch. Hard work, but I pay seven bucks an hour under the table. Know anybody lookin to make some extra Christmas money?"

"Might have trouble findin anyone willin to do it in this godawful weather. Snow's gotten heavy early this year."

"Yeah, that's exactly why I need the help."

"I'll try and get the word out. You can put a flyer on the wood board if you want to."

"Thanks, Russ."

Two more customers came in and Russ went off to greet them. Tom's plates were slid under him and he gobbled up the grub with the greed of his livestock. He wanted to stay at the diner a little longer to enjoy the warmth and chat with the locals, but he didn't have time and couldn't think of anything he really wanted to say to anyone. His mind was on the drifter again when he knew he should be focusing on the day's work. The man's face rebounded off the corners of his mind, pale and threatening, refusing to give him peace.

CHAPTER FIVE

The wind was angry. It came at him like the breath of a dragon, burning his exposed cheeks and fingertips. Tom wore the gloves with the fingers cut off so he could manipulate the chicken wire better as he mended the coop, the very same wind having bent it out of shape.

At the feed store, Tom and Ed Green had talked about hired help and how both of them were in need. Ed had lost a full-time employee on short notice, a longhaired hippie who'd decided to move to Burlington. This left Ed to pull longer hours to save on paying overtime to his staff.

"Try workin outside in the winter before you start to cryin," Tom joked.

"Hey, I did my time wranglin and you know it."

As a young man he'd worked as a cowpuncher and had taken a part-time job at Tom's ranch one summer. Now he was the proprietor of his own business, selling feed, rope, propane, boots, guns, ammo, and more. Vermont was good about keeping out big corporations like Walmart, so Ed was able to stay in business, but the stress of running the store had taken a toll on him. Though he had bushy hair on the sides of his head, he was bald on top and had developed a paunch over the past few years. His posture was now hunched whereas once he'd been strapping and had more confidence in his stride. Something about Ed looked pained and defeated now, as if his business, marriage and three kids had been a heavy load he'd had no wagon for, the emotional weight so daunting that it had actually bowed his body. Though Tom had over twenty years on the man, whenever he saw Ed he found himself feeling grateful to not look as beaten as he did.

"Kids today," Ed complained. "Time was they'd be walkin down the street on snowy days like this, carryin shovels and lookin to clear out driveways and make a few bucks. Where are they now, huh? Playin video games their mommies and daddies bought em for doin nothin. That's what. Takin a hundred stupid-ass pictures of themselves so they can put em on the Facebook. Remember when kids used to keep diaries and got mad when someone read it? Well now they post all that shit online and get mad when people *don't* read it!"

It was the same thing Tom thought but never said out loud for fear of sounding like an old man. Yet here was Ed, just over forty, coming off like Ebenezer Scrooge in a pair of overalls.

"Times have changed," Tom agreed. "No doubt there."

"Changed for the worse, I say."

As Ed took his elbows off the counter, Tom noticed the fresh weight the big man had put on, all of it in the belly, and almost made a comment about the old holiday spread but decided against it. He found he was biting his tongue more often these days.

Tom changed the subject. "Well, I'm gonna need three big bags of senior feed and one of the regular. Some sugar cubes and alfalfa pellets too. And I could use a replacement impeller for my paddle pump."

"Decko Bronze, right?"

"Ayuh."

"I've got plenty of feed and treats but the impeller will take a day or two. Think you can get a few days' worth out of the old one with some lubricant in the discharge ports?"

Tom shrugged. "Replacement's overdue, but I figure I can push it a little further."

They promised each other to keep an eye out for hired hands and one of the stock boys helped Tom load the feed into his truck. He headed back to the ranch, fed the horses and cattle, and started the day's general maintenance of the grounds, cleaning out the stalls and buckets. Jep tailed alongside him like a second shadow, good about not getting in the way while never straying too far. The dog needed a job, mental and physical exercise, but Tom wasn't offering either at the moment. There was too much to do.

Slate clouds hovered motionless like chunks of clay, even as the wind whirled, cutting as mean as rusty razors. He didn't want to plant his knees in the snow, so he squatted as he worked, knees sounding like sandpaper, feeling a strain in his lower back that had become an all too familiar nemesis. Even the chicken wire wasn't cooperating. It danced away from his fingers in favor of the wind.

Tom cursed. He'd long thought that by this point in life he'd have permanent help he could afford. It pained him to be staring at a future without retirement. Once he got too old to do all this work he wasn't sure how he would get by. He'd probably have to sell the land he and Betty had worked so hard on all these years, and the thought of doing so pained him even more. But even the roughest rancher couldn't wrangle and ride into his golden years. Eventually the cowboy life was bound to buck you.

Once he got the fencing in place he decided to give himself a rest to warm up in the house, but when he got inside he realized he was running late for the bus stop. The day had slipped away from him and school had let out some forty-five minutes ago. He dashed to his truck and was just barely out of the driveway when Mrs. MacDougall's car came down the road.

Once again he cursed under his breath. It was bad enough to have lost track of time when the kid was concerned without the shame of her best friend's parent picking up his slack. He got out of the truck, trying to think of a good excuse, wondering if he should even bother or just admit that he hadn't checked his watch in a while. This forgetfulness made him feel incredibly old.

The car pulled up and he spotted Fay MacDougall at the wheel, a pinched look of concern on her face. Frost made the window struggle as it lowered.

"Everything all right, Tom?"

She was younger than Tom's own children, a soccer mom who had a phony pleasantry about her, as if she wanted to keep all the world on her side so badly that she didn't dare get too close to it, leaving all her relationships an act and putting up an artificial imprint that hovered before her like a force field. Her expensive car and clothing, as well as the glimmering rock on her finger, served to announce her to the world as something better than it: a shimmering, well-kept thing of bought beauty.

"Just got a little held up," he said. "I was headin to the stop right now."

"Well, I was surprised when Paige said she had no cell phone to call you." Fay tried to pass off her judgement as playful nudging. "She wanted to borrow mine to call the house but I figured I'd just drive her on over."

Tom tipped his hat. "Much obliged."

The back door opened and Paige jumped out. He was worried she would give him the evil eye for his delay but she seemed neutral, unfazed, and somehow that was worse.

Paige waved, her loose mitten flapping. "Bye Alice. Bye Mrs. MacDougall. Thank you for the ride."

At least she's polite, Tom thought.

"Anytime," MacDougall said.

Tom took Paige's hand, as if this would prove to little miss Fay MacDougall that he was a caring grandfather after all, as if he had something to prove to this woman he barely knew.

"Thanks again." He guided Paige up into the truck and closed her door. "Stay warm."

The woman smiled, all pink lipstick and blush, and as she pulled away Tom saw Alice waving, showing off a smile that was almost as big and irritating as her mother's.

CHAPTER SIX

On Friday morning, Tom headed into town to identify a man caught panhandling outside of Buddy's Bar and Grill. He was picked up the night before and Dale called Tom first thing in the morning. He didn't really have any charges to press, but Dale wanted to know if this was the same man who'd been caught snooping around the farmhouse. It would give the sheriff all the more reason to run the bum out of town.

Driving over the lake, Tom could only see a few feet of bridge in front of him. Dense fog breathed above the water, thick and blinding, making him feel like he had entered another dimension. Even when he crossed all the way over, the streets of the quaint downtown district were lost in the undulating, white mist, so he drove slowly with the truck's overhead lights on. Once at the station he hurried inside, weirdly unnerved by the fog, as if pirate ghosts were going to lunge at him from behind the rolling grey. He shrugged it off as nerves but was still relieved to get inside.

Dale took him to a dimly lit room in the back with a two-way mirror in it, on the other side of which sat the man who called himself Jason. He was sitting in a chair, leaning on a small table and smoking a cigarette. He looked like he hadn't slept in days. He was in a stained t-shirt and Tom could see the man's forearms. They were covered in small cuts like he'd been trying to drown a cat. Under the unflattering fluorescents, the man looked yellowed, sickly and worn, a weaker man than the one who'd been in Tom's yard just the other night. But it was the same man; of that Tom had no doubt.

Dale shook Tom's hand. "Thanks for comin down to the station."

"You betcha. So what happens to our new friend now?"

"Well, we could charge him with vagrancy, but..."

"Vagrancy? You mean you can charge a man with bein homeless?"

"If he's creatin a disturbance. He's been askin for money on the stoop of Buddy's place, and Buddy ain't happy about it. He stopped servin the guy but he wouldn't leave. Not to mention the snoopin around your ranch. Plus, he's got priors."

"What'd he do?"

"Small stuff, you know; petty theft, possession of grass. He's pretty lit right now, so he'll spend the night in our drunk tank. But after that I'll probably just let him go."

Tom sighed. "Well, shit, Dale. Then why'd you want me to come up here and see him for?"

"'Cause now we can turn the screws on him. It'll spook the punk to find out we know he was wanderin around your house. We can use that to run his ass outta town."

"But no arrest?"

"It'd be different if we caught him in the act. As is, all we really have is public drunkenness, but that's only against the law if he's endangerin anyone or their property. He'd pay a $500 dollar fine if we slapped him with it, but that's it. You really wanna pursue a trespassin charge?"

Tom shook his head. "Naw, doesn't seem worth the hassle. I have too much work to do to be in and outta court. Besides, I think he was just stoned."

Dale sucked his teeth. "I'm gonna run him off then. He's gonna know that he ain't welcome here no more."

⊱

That afternoon, Tom and Paige took the horses for a ride around the ranch. It was a cold Friday with no sun, the land looking as grey and hard as a stone knife hone, and the skeletal tree line of the valley was still and somber, their lifeless melancholy reminding Tom of the tranquility of graves.

He wanted to show Paige how to herd the cattle and spot the signs they gave when they were in trouble, but she seemed irritable, so he settled for what he hoped would be a relaxing ride. He felt obligated to chip away at the girl's silent pain, blanketing her against its chill with all the kindness and understanding he had to offer.

He rode Essie and Paige used the stepping block to get onto Hondo's back—a draft horse pony Tom sometimes used to make extra cash at birthday parties when the little horse wasn't dragging carts in the field. He was a white-coated pony, slightly peppered, and stubborn when it came to stopping and chewing on bentgrass. But Paige liked him and that was enough for Tom.

Not even ten minutes into the ride, she said: "I want to go back to the house."

"We'll just ride over the hill and back. Won't take but half an hour." He saw her face darken. "What, you too cold?"

"No. I just want to go back to my room. I want to be alone."

"Something happen at school?"

She didn't answer.

"You can talk to your old granddad."

"You keep saying that. What would you know about my problems?"

Tom blinked with surprise. "You know, honey, smart asses don't fit into saddles. Besides, believe it or not I was your age once, back when we hid in caves when the thunder groaned and wild buffalo ruled the Earth. Ain't no kinda trouble I ain't seen and lived through."

"I don't want to talk about anything. I just want to go back."

His shoulders slumped. He understood that these bouts of depression were normal, but they still perturbed him, especially when he was trying to strengthen his bond with her.

"Well, how about you just humor me for half an hour and then I won't bug you for the rest of the night."

She exhaled, her body deflating. "Fine."

"It's good for little girls to get fresh air and be out in nature. There's so little of it nowadays, and even less time for it."

Hondo stopped and started chewing on a tuft of grass that hung limply from a rise. Paige didn't cluck to the pony or kick his sides. She just sat there and let him chew. Tom almost told her how to get the pony moving again, but she knew how, and he knew what she was telling him even if she'd given up on words.

"Alright then," he said.

They turned back.

~

Once the sun began to set, Tom went inside and shook out of his boots and coat. He hung his hat above his father's lucky horseshoe and went into the kitchen. He hadn't planned dinner, so he would have to get creative. He'd been considering assigning dinner as one of Paige's new chores on weekends, but wasn't going to press it while she was in such a sour mood. Still, it seemed like she was in a sour mood more often than not.

He'd been thinking of calling Mary, but he hadn't talked to his sister-in-law in quite a while. There was no negativity between them, but after losing Betty, he slowly fell out of touch with her side of the family. Tom needed a woman's advice now though.

Is it normal for today's young girls to be this way? Paige had a great deal more weighing her down than most children. But the thought that her behavior might be related to some sort of hormonal change crossed his mind. *She's not even eleven yet; she can't really be changing that way already, can she?* He wasn't ready for picking up tampons at the grocery store and having the sex talk with his granddaughter. He'd left that to Betty when Dawn had gotten her first period, and he'd only talked to his son about sex after he'd caught him naked with a girl he'd snuck into his room when he was fifteen. The thought of Paige going through early puberty gave him the chills. He didn't know how he was going to handle it on his own. He was having enough trouble handling things as it was.

He decided to call Mary once Paige was in bed.

His granddaughter seemed a little brighter as she came into the kitchen, and even gave him a small, apologetic smile. He put his arm out and she came into him for a hug, causing his heart to swell like a busted lip.

Her voice was soft and low. "Sorry I'm a butthead."

He laughed. "Aw, honey."

She sighed into his chest, a hatchling in his arms.

"You sure there ain't nothin you want to talk to me about, darlin?"

"No, I'm okay. I just didn't feel well earlier."

He put a hand to her forehand. "Gettin sick?"

"No, not that kind of not feeling well. Just weird and kind of tired. Not sleepy tired, just tired of everything."

"Well, I guess we all get that way sometimes. No harm done."

He looked into her eyes and they were just as dark as Essie's or Hondo's, only hers were blank like those of a doll. Most people's eyes were the windows of the soul, as the saying goes, but Paige's were more like a closed, metal door with a bar across it. He wondered what was really going on behind them. Searching her face for answers, it occurred to him that he rarely saw the girl smile wider than a smirk.

"Can I ask you something?"

She nodded.

"Christmas gotcha down?"

For Halloween, Paige and Alice had dressed up and Fay took them into town for the costume party and trick 'r treating. Paige had only gotten excited about wearing a costume when she and Alice decided to go as fairy princesses like the ones they always drew pictures of. While not as jovial as he would have liked to see her, Paige had at least participated.

When it came to Thanksgiving, it was a quiet affair, the two of them being on their own. Tom made a turkey breast and instant mashed potatoes, and they spent most of the day lounging around the house like it was just another Sunday. Paige hadn't seemed distraught on the surface, but she was rather quiet and didn't show any interest in watching the parade. It seemed the more family-oriented holidays made her sink inward, retreating into her grey vortex.

She took a minute, thinking it over. "No. It doesn't get me down. Not really."

"Not really also means *yeah, a little*."

"But Christmas is a happy time."

"Well, sometimes people put a little too much pressure on everyone to be happy at Christmas, and that makes it harder to enjoy it. All the movies and such set the standard too high." He wondered if he was talking above her head. "You know, just because everyone else says somethin is fun, that don't mean you gotta think it is. You decide what's fun, darlin, nobody else."

She was quiet for a moment. "Okay."

Their hug ended and Tom got up to start on dinner.

"Wanna help me peel some potatoes?"

"Sure."

As he emptied them out of the bowl she looked up at him with those paralyzing eyes of hers. The corners of her mouth were pinched, and in that moment she looked so much like Dawn had as a child that Tom nearly gasped.

"Christmas doesn't make me sad," she said. "I just don't care about it. There's no Santa and there's no Jesus. There are no miracles either. It's all a big lie. So why be happy about it?"

Tom was taken back. He'd never heard such cynicism from a child before. It took a slice of his heart and twisted, ringing it out like a wet rag.

"Why do you say all that?"

"'Cause it's true. It's all lies."

The saddest part of it was she was right. Tom had been raised a Christian but had turned his back on religion long ago. He'd seen too much death and suffering to stay a believer. He didn't know what he believed now, but angels and miracles and an afterlife floating on cloud recliners certainly wasn't part of it. Dawn and her husband Leon had never been altogether too religious, but he didn't think they would have filled their daughter's head with such aggressive atheism, especially not pertaining to Christmas, which was really a holiday for children above all else. What had made Paige so hostile toward it?

Something about a child not believing in miracles was just so devastating.

He didn't believe much in magic or miracles either. The only results he'd ever seen came from back sweat and sore muscles. They came from dedication and work so hard you could barely climb the stairs at night. If Christmas really brought miracles, then his son Scott would return the calls he made every year. And if Jesus couldn't see to it to keep Tom's wife and daughter alive, then the Lord could only be indifferent, sadistic or imaginary.

But Tom was an old man. He'd had six times as long as his granddaughter to have the pain of being alive grind him down to a grey nub. Paige was just a little girl, an ewe in the field just beginning to graze, black sheep or not. Such cynicism had no place in a mind that innocent, but who could blame her after what she'd endured. At ten years old, Paige had had her youth cut short by tragedy, and was forced to face hard truths about life and death. No wonder she couldn't enjoy a little Christmas make-believe.

"I'm right, aren't I?" she asked. "You don't believe in all that stuff, do you?"

Her eyes were challenging. Clearly she was hoping he'd agree so she could maintain respect for him.

"No," he admitted. "Of course not."

"Then that's it."

She took one of the potatoes from him and drew open the drawer for a knife. She held it upright, looking at her elongated reflection in the blade.

"I make my own stories," she said. "I don't need anybody else's. It's like you said—I decide what's fun, not somebody else."

They prepared dinner in silence.

～✕～

With Paige upstairs in bed, Tom sat in his armchair, looking out the window at the tumbling snow as it blanketed the valley. He thought about the lease he had on most of his acres and stressed over the Red Brangus cow that had fallen ill beyond the vet's repair last month, her death taking away more money than Tom could afford to lose. He worried about falling further back on his Farmer Mac loan. He kept telling himself the money would come if he continued to invest in the ranch and put hard work into it. It always had before. It wouldn't help him to worry over the big picture when he had details to worry about first and foremost. There were squeeze chutes to work on and he needed a new titling table. The corral needed more preparation for the harsh winter months ahead that were always so cruel to northern New England.

And then there was Paige.

He lifted the phone from its cradle on the end table, close to pressing the autodial number that had Mary's name on it. He held the receiver in his hand tighter than he needed to, hearing the plastic creak, but couldn't bring himself to hit the button. Somehow even thinking about talking to Mary stirred up too many thoughts of Betty, and how bad things had been in the end, thoughts he did not want to be reminded of.

He had enough on his mind as it was.

Placing the phone back in the cradle, Tom sipped his seltzer, wishing it were alcohol, but not really.

CHAPTER SEVEN

On Saturday morning Paige went off to play with Alice, taking her glittery notebook with her. She bolted out the door so quickly that Tom had to remind her to put on her coat. He watched her walk down the trail as she entered the long rows of oaks between the ranch and Fletcher Street where the MacDougalls lived.

It was good to see her excited to play. He wished she was as happy to spend time with him as she was to spend it with Alice, but he would take whatever happiness he could get. Tom believed kids would never grow up if they weren't allowed a little freedom, so he was fine with Paige playing in the woods with her friend. It gave her the fresh air and exercise she so desperately needed in the winter months when the monkey bars on the playground were too cold to touch and the lake was frozen over so you couldn't swim.

Once she was behind the tree line, Tom went to work on chopping more wood. He had logs from a fallen yellow birch, and he took some of them out of the barn and carried them to the block. It was a large sugar maple stump that he had fitted with a tire to hold the logs as he split them. He swung the axe, feeling his shoulders grind, his arms groaning like an old boat on troubled waters. Aggressive heat crept up his neck like spiders, but he kept on chopping, glad to at least still be strong enough to cut straight through the logs with one swing. Despite his age he got a lot of exercise maintaining the ranch. It kept him in good shape, and the muscle memory from his younger days as a boxer, and briefly as a soldier, helped him maintain mass. His heart was tough and his body was sinewy for a man his age, especially now that he ate better to keep his blood pressure down and had gone off the booze.

He spent the early morning moving the cattle and maintaining the barn, switching out propane tanks and taking care of the supplemental feeding, tossing out some of the straw that had gotten wet. There was a softball-sized hole in one side of the barn where the snow had seeped in. He would have to repair it before the day was through. Where the fields weren't snowy they were muddy, and all the earth was cold and unyielding. Black birds bleated in the ashen sky, darting as one into the cloaking trees while the woods echoed the wind like a massive, breathing animal, the gusts coming slow but consistent.

Tom moved across the land, as much a part of this valley as the hills that lapped each other like waves—as much cowboy as his worn boots and sun-bleached Stetson, as much a shadow of an old way of life as a bullet-riddled flag or an ice truck rusting on an overgrown lawn. Atop Essie, Tom rounded the herd, telling the horse things he didn't share with anyone else.

"She's a sad girl, my granddaughter. At least I think she's sad. Sometimes it's not like she's depressed though. It's not like she feels anyways particular at all. That's what worries me, old girl. It's like her emotions are just turned off. But that's normal with trauma, right?"

The horse snorted mist, picking up its pace as Tom nudged its ribs to direct the herd toward the stalls.

"I just wish I knew how to—"

A shrill scream tore out of the woods, a terrible cry that rippled his skin. Essie started, rustling the cattle. They fluttered about, twitching, skittish. Tom put his heels into the horse and she galloped toward the trail, entering its long throat, the dead trees whizzing past him in a black blur. Tom swallowed hard.

That was a little girl's scream.

✕

He found her in the woods.

Yesterday's fog had dissipated but the thicket clung to its remnants. Paige emerged from the smoky trees like a fox running from a pack of dogs, her face a sickly pale. At first she didn't notice him, too focused on running. She skidded to a halt when the horse came into her view, slipping in the snow but jumping right back up. Paige shot glances in all directions as Tom dismounted. He rushed to his granddaughter.

"Baby, are you all right? What's goin on? Where's Alice?"

She wouldn't look at him. Her eyes stayed on the forest, watching the trees, fog and snow, as if waiting for something terrible. She was unnervingly silent.

"Talk to me, Paige!"

He grabbed her chin, tilting it up so she faced him. Her eyes were withered coals, her chin dimpled from a clenched jaw.

"It's Alice," she said.

He waited for more.

"She's back there," she said, pointing off the trail. "I think she's

30

dead."

The world seemed to spin away from Tom's feet. His throat turned to sandpaper, making it difficult to get out the words. "What? What happened?"

She shook her head and stared at the ground. He tilted her chin up again.

"What happened, Paige?"

"I want to go home."

"Take me to her, right now."

"I just want to go home, Grandpa."

"You just told me you think Alice is *dead*! Now come on, take me to her. She needs our help."

Paige shook her head. "We can't help her."

"Baby, we have to get to her right away, now come on."

He nudged her and they started toward the brush.

"Did she have an accident?" he asked. "What happened?"

Paige pushed through dead shrubs and Tom led Essie over them. They were off the trail now, trenching through snow and suckering roots. Icy, black twigs rose out of the snow like a coarse coat of hair and grabbed at their ankles. For a moment the hemlock trees grew denser. Then they began to space out, curling teeth in a rotting jack-o-lantern. They gave way to a clearing where gray nothingness made a shallow bowl in the earth.

In the center of it was Alice.

She was lying on her stomach in the packed snow, her head facing away from them.

She wasn't moving.

"Dear God…" Tom ran to the little girl. "Alice? Alice!"

She didn't respond. As he reached her he crouched down, feeling Paige's silent presence right behind him. His hand shook as he reached for the little girl's shoulder.

He turned her over.

Now it was his scream that ripped through the valley.

CHAPTER EIGHT

"There was a man…" Paige was saying.

She sounded so far away, like she was on the other end of a phone call with a bad connection, calling from another planet.

Blood was everywhere.

Alice's white coat was soused in crimson. On her chest and stomach were wounds, blood so thick it was purple. It seemed she'd been stabbed several times. Her face was as white as the snow that cradled her skull in a powdery halo, and her eyes stared off lifelessly, half open, blind.

Tom checked her pulse.

Nothing.

He let out a small cry and hunched over, horror crushing him into the cold earth below. Had his stomach not been empty, he would have vomited. He forced his breath to stay steady so not to hyperventilate.

"A man?" he managed to ask.

Paige nodded, still looking around the woods. "He came out of the bushes and attacked us. He had a big knife, like a butcher knife."

Tom fought against the shock that threatened to anchor him. All he had to defend them was his pocketknife and he didn't want to have a knife fight with some blade-wielding maniac. He had to get Paige back to the safety of the house, get his shotgun, and call Dale to get the police out here. He didn't want to leave Alice's body in case the killer might take her, but he didn't want to disrupt the crime scene and damage any evidence. Most of all he just wanted to get them out of those woods. There was a deep sense of dread here, the likes of which he had not felt since the war.

"I want to go home, Grandpa. Please."

He stood up, clutching her tiny hand. "Come on."

Tom boosted her onto Essie's back, untied the horse, and swung into the saddle in a way he hadn't in twenty years—one quick, spinning lunge. He thrust his heels into Essie's ribs and they took off in a gallop, the cold indifference of the winter wind forcing the tears from his eyes.

He thought about going back to the woods—to look for footprints or at least to guard the body—but he couldn't risk leaving Paige alone, not even locked in the house. Dale wasn't at the station when Tom called, but Deputy Cooper Struve and two more officers were heading out to the scene, telling Tom the sheriff would be notified right away.

The seventeen minutes it took for the first car to arrive felt like seventeen days. Struve pulled up with another officer and they got out of the cruiser in a hurry. Tom met them in the driveway. The look on the deputy's face told Tom that he hadn't dealt with anything like this before, and Tom pitied the man for what he was about to see.

"How far?" Struve asked.

"About ten minutes on foot."

"Let's go."

"Should one of us wait for Dale?"

Struve's eyes darted, lost. "Ummm. No. We can radio our position. The medical examiner will be here soon too. So will the photographer. You said you didn't touch anything, right?"

"Nothin. I turned her over to find a pulse, but that was it."

The officers trenched toward the woods and Tom got Paige from the house. He didn't want her to see her friend's body again, but there would be a lot of questions to ask, and he didn't want to leave her alone. Who knew if the man who'd killed Alice was still out here.

Paige moaned. "Please. I don't want to go back."

"I know, honey, but I need you to stick with me right now, and the police will need to ask you about what happened."

"I already told you."

"You need to tell the story to them, Paige. The whole story, so they can catch this bad man."

The four of them walked down the trail in relative silence. Tom had offered to saddle up Essie and the pony but the officers declined. Struve didn't know how to ride.

When they reached the woods, it seemed colder now, an arctic grove with dark secrets. Tom kept one hand on Paige's shoulder while the other carried the shotgun. The deputies were on high alert too, necks snapping toward the slightest rustle in the brush, sensitive to so much as a bird's chirp. When they reached the clearing the silence was as heavy as an anvil.

Deputy Struve gasped. "My God…"

Alice was where they'd left her, only now the snow around her body was bright red. Tom pulled Paige in close to him, tucking her face into the side of his belly. She pressed into him, tucking her arms. The officers circled the dead girl's body for a moment and Struve drew his gun, watching the woods with a pale grimace. The other lawman noted the time, speaking code to dispatch through the receiver on his shoulder. Beyond the woods, sirens cried like banshees.

"The ambulance is on its way. So is the coroner." The lawman looked at Paige, then back at Tom. "We're going to have to keep you separate for questioning, just so you don't get each other confused."

"Alright. But I'm not letting her out of my sight right now."

With gun drawn, Struve made a sweep of the area. Tom heard other voices coming from the beginning of the trail and went back and waved the sheriff over. Two paramedics followed Dale, and there were three troopers with him, two of which carried pump-action shotguns.

When Dale reached the scene, he ordered his men to rope it off with police tape and had them comb the surrounding woods. Within the next twenty minutes the sketch artist and photographer arrived, along with the medical examiner, all of which surrounded Alice's body as the officers continued their search and secured the area. A man began picking up tiny articles with tweezers and placing them into plastic bags while the paramedics went to the ambulance and came back with a gurney. When Tom saw the body bag he twitched, slugged by the finality of it.

Dale was already haggard.

"Jesus, Tom."

Down at the station another officer took Paige into a room alone to talk to her, and Dale brought Tom into his office to do the same. Dale had him go through the story twice, telling him to make sure he didn't forget any details, no matter how small they might seem. Tom told him everything, which he felt wasn't much at all.

"So she told you a man came out of the bushes and attacked them."

"Ayuh."

"She say what he looked like?"

"No. She just wanted to get outta them woods."

"Makes sense for her to be scared."

Tom thought she had seemed more shocked than frightened, but didn't mention it.

"Helluva thing," Dale said. "It gets you to thinkin."

Tom expected more but Dale fell quiet.

"What're you thinkin?" Tom asked.

"About your visitor. I'm sure he's sprung to your mind, hasn't he?"

"That he did."

In fact, Tom had been thinking about it since he'd seen Alice's body, but he didn't want to throw it up to the police because it was just a layman's suspicion.

Dale rubbed his chin. "A man is found snoopin around your ranch and then the girls are attacked in the woods right behind it."

"I'm guessin he's not in your jail anymore?"

"Nope. Let him out yesterday. Told him to get the hell outta our little town and stay out, but that was the end of it." Dale shook his head. "But she didn't say what he looked like?"

"No, but I didn't ask her too much. I just wanted to get her safe and call you."

"It's okay. Sergeant Cole is with her now. He's got a way with kids. Gets answers from them while still being gentle."

"That's good to hear. I'm worried about how all this is gonna affect her, Dale. Real worried. Losing her parents is enough to destroy a child. Now she's lost a friend too…"

The men sighed as one.

"I know a good lady shrink," Dale said. "Works with traumatized kids. She oughta be able to help Paige out."

Tom flinched at the thought of psychiatry, but he'd needed help even before today's tragedy. "I should've found her a head shrinker from the get go. Maybe it would've helped her talk about things. Lord knows I've never been good at gettin her to open up."

Dale flipped through his Rolodex, found the right card, and handed it to him.

"You might want to talk to someone too," Dale said. "No matter how much you see in war, seeing a little girl like that will always tear a man up inside."

Tom wondered who had the terrible job of telling Alice's parents but didn't ask about it. The less he knew about what the MacDougalls had to go through, the better he'd sleep. He'd buried a daughter of his own, but as grievous as it had been, at least she was full grown when she died, and the accident was not comparable to this senseless butchery.

Dale shook his head. "Still haven't found no murder weapon neither."

Tom slumped in the chair. "So what happens now?"

"There's a lot more people to question: neighbors, friends, family. My boys are going over every inch of the hillocks. Hopefully they find somethin in those woods. The bastard may be long gone and may've taken the murder weapon with him. And now with how heavy the snow's comin down we might have trouble with footprints."

Tom blinked. "Shit, Dale. You sayin he's gonna get away?"

"Not exactly, just sayin it's lookin like an uphill battle is all."

There was a knock at the door.

"Come in."

The tall black man who'd taken Paige in for questioning stuck his head through the door.

"How'd we do, Deontay?"

"Good," said Sergeant Deontay Cole. "Sure enough, we've put out an APB on the drunk who was in here the other day." He looked at Tom and nodded. "According to your girl, that same creeper came back to your ranch."

✕

Paige's story was a chilling one.

The two girls were playing in the woods when the man who had appeared in her grandfather's yard just a few nights before came bursting out of the bushes, telling them he was going to rape and kill them both. When they started to run, he grabbed Alice by the hair. Paige had looked back as he was jabbing a butcher knife into Alice's stomach. Paige screamed at the top of her lungs, hoping someone would hear her and come to their aid. Tom got to her before she was fully out of the woods, and when they came back to the clearing Alice was dead; her killer, vanished.

"I think she's in shock," Deontay said. "She had trouble opening up at first, but we got the story. Now she seems numb."

"Of course she's in shock!" Tom said. "She's ten-goddamned-years old. Hell, I'm an old man and I'm in shock myself."

"I mean clinical shock, sir—psychological shock."

Dale stepped forward. "I can get you a rushed appointment with that doctor, Tom. Paige might need some medication."

Tom looked at both men.

"It's very common," Deontay said. "Children tend to react this way to something like this. They don't know how to handle it, so they crawl inward. It'll take time for her to sort it out."

Tom pinched the bridge of his nose. "As if she hasn't been through enough."

Deontay looked to Dale, who explained.

"Mr. Hargrave here is her grandfather *and* her guardian too."

The sergeant nodded, a touch of mourning in his eyes. He ran his hand over his shaven head.

"So," Dale said, "she's sure it was the same man?"

Deontay nodded. "That's what she says."

"But she's *sure*? She got a good look at him both times?"

"First she gave a description that matched, then I had Rita pull up his photo along with a few other white males his age with sandy hair. She picked Reston out of them."

Dale turned to Tom. "You think she got a good look at him that night he was in your yard?"

"Suppose she could've from the window. I was too busy with him to notice."

Dale took a moment, sipped his coffee. "Well, the bum was on foot when we picked him up. No car. Unless he hitched, he can't have gotten far, though he'd be extra stupid to stick around now."

"Yeah," said Deontay.

"Has the family been notified?"

Tom tensed, thinking of Alice's mother. He'd always been irked by Fay's smug smile. Now he thought the poor woman might never smile again, and that was much worse.

"Yes, sir. Struve went out there with Sadler. The mother was home."

Dale grimaced. "I've been sheriff of this county for fifteen years, and a part of this police force for twenty-seven, and I've never had a child-murder like this. Never. We've had a few instances of neglect that led to a child's death, and accidents, includin some drunk drivin deaths. But never the cold-blooded murder of a little girl. Makes me wonder just what's happenin to our quiet town."

Tom had no reply to this. Neither did the sergeant. The three men were silent then, as silent as cowering animals.

CHAPTER NINE

Paige's name wasn't mentioned in the local news report. She was referred to as *another local girl*. The mug shot of Jason Reston, the drifter, came on screen several times, his haggard face reminding Tom of bus stations and free clinics. He looked sickly, more junkie than murderer, but there was something in his stare, a depravity beyond drug addiction. The mental image of the man stabbing Alice raked across Tom's mind. He tried to shake it away, but it kept circling back, jabbing and tireless.

Paige was in her room now and he wasn't sure if he should let her have the time to herself or check in and try to talk with her about what happened. She'd been silent and half-awake all afternoon. Tom wondered if the pills the shrink had given her were making her drowsy or if it was an after effect of post-traumatic stress. If she were sleeping in her room he didn't want to disturb her.

She'd spent an hour alone with Dr. White before Tom was invited in for an additional half hour. White then held a fifteen-minute session with both of them, and then another fifteen alone with Tom so she could fill him in on what she'd observed with Paige. White didn't say much more than Sergeant Cole had. Paige was in shock and it would take time for her to fully process what had happened, and even longer to cope with it.

She explained the stages Paige would go through, including denial, anger, and depression, and that the stages could come in any order. Some of these stages could be long lasting; others, rushed. It all seemed like generalizations to Tom, just wild guesses that anyone could make, but he paid attention and nodded respectfully when the doctor spoke.

Afterward he had filled Paige's prescription and bought her a can of juice to take her first dose on the way home. He even got her a Twix, her favorite candy. Even though he was already behind, he decided to let the rest of his chores wait until the following day so he could stay in the house to be available for her at any moment. The ranch needed him, but his granddaughter needed him more.

Finally, he called Mary.

"Hello?"

Her voice went through him in an afterglow.

"Mary. It's Tom."

There was a pause. "My goodness. Tom. How nice to hear from you."

He wasn't sure how to begin. "How are things?"

"Good, good."

He asked about her husband David and his nephews. Mary and David had been at Dawn's funeral, but Tom's nephews hadn't shown. He judged them harshly for it, as he did his own son for not making an appearance. It was one thing for Scott to be estranged from his father and not want to see him, but it was another not to pay his respects to his little sister and only sibling. But Scott's behavior had never made much sense.

The two of them never had much in common. Scott hated horses and ranching and cursed his chores, jumping at the chance to move out the moment he turned eighteen. He didn't like sports and he hated New England. From what Tom could tell the only things his son had liked was heavy metal music and pot, and as he'd grown older his interests changed to isolation and grudges. He never married—never even kept a girlfriend for very long—and he was very distant from the entire family even though his resentment was exclusive to his old man, blaming him for his neglected upbringing and refusing to forgive Tom for his past troubles with alcohol. He had resented his mother for what he considered being apathetic about the issue, though Tom knew that was not the case. Scott seemed to alienate himself from his sister, aunt and cousins just because of association.

Had things been different, Paige might have been left in Scott's care, but Dawn knew how bitter and solipsistic her brother was and felt that her father was the better candidate. She'd seen how much her father had changed since their younger years, and how he'd conquered his alcoholism—like her mother, she had a large heart that was open to forgiveness. Tom knew he'd failed her just the same as he had Scott, but his daughter never abandoned him or rubbed his past mistakes into his face.

Tom had never been physically abusive. His drinking made him sloppy, neglectful, and an embarrassment to his family, but it didn't make him violent. Dawn understood that he'd struggled with an addiction, and was proud of him for pulling through and making amends. She'd been there with him to help take care of her mother when the cancer was taking her, and they'd formed an even stronger bond because of it. While special, the bond had come far too late and was all too short-lived. Tom blamed himself for that, amongst other things.

"How's Paige?" Mary asked.

"Not so good." Then he told her why.

He wasn't sure what to say or how to say it, so he just started at the beginning and let it flow naturally. He told her everything and she listened, never interrupting, absorbing it all.

"Oh my God, Tom," she said when he'd finished. "We saw it on the news but never dreamed it was... I mean, my God. Is she okay?"

"She is physically, but psychologically we think she's in shock. She's always been quiet and sorta withdrawn, even before Dawn's accident, but now... well, you can imagine. Took her to a shrink. A real nice lady. Says she's gonna go through these stages. Says it's all normal, but it sure don't feel right to me, or at least not good. I don't know what to do with all this, Mary. I was hopin you could sorta help me figure this out, give me a woman's perspective the way Betty woulda."

He heard her shuffle and knew the sentiment warmed her. He'd always liked Mary. She was the one person from Betty's family who treated him with decency. He felt merely tolerated by the others and generally disliked by her old man, who had wanted his daughter to marry a banker or a doctor, not some muddy-boots cowpuncher. Mary had been Betty's closest sibling, and the youngest of the three sisters. She was a good sister-in-law to have, and he wondered why he didn't talk to her more often. He guessed it just seemed weird to do so now that Betty was gone, as though by dying she divorced him from her family.

"I've never dealt with anything like this," she said. "I think it's best to do what the doctor says. It makes sense that she'll be in shock and go through those stages and all."

"I suppose. It ain't just this whole mess though. She's been withdrawn and whatnot for some time. I don't know if it's just a normal reaction to so much misery or if it's somethin I should worry about."

"Who's to say what's normal? She's still struggling with her parents gone and adjusting to her new life with you."

"Ayuh."

"These things take time."

"You know, she finally had a friend in that poor girl, and now this." He immediately regretted how selfish that sounded. "I mean, you know, it's tragic is what I mean."

"I know what you mean."

A silence fell between them.

"So what do I do?" he asked.

"Just what you're already doing. Be there for her and be patient."

"I always will be."

"Of course you will. You're a good man Tom, and I have no doubt that you'll be a good guardian to her as well as a grandpa."

PART TWO

WHILE SHEPHERDS WATCHED
THEIR FLOCKS

CHAPTER TEN

Days passed.

The police had yet to find Reston or uncover a murder weapon, but his face was on every telephone pole and appeared on the nightly news. A heavy gloom fell over the town that was more than just the grey clouds that lay motionless over the valley.

Tom worked in the fields and kept Paige home from school for the time being. The horses hung their heads while shaggy cattle snorted in disgust. Even they were sluggish, as if the animals too were mourning the loss of an innocent girl and the farewell to a once safe and simple town. And when Tom would ride past the wooded trail in the basin every day, he'd look at the tangle of dead trees on the slope, knowing that just beyond them was a grove were little Alice MacDougall's body had laid, her stomach shredded, her mouth curled in a frown, teeth bloodstained.

He let his mind wander to other sadness and focused on the busted fencing and December air that stabbed at him as he battled uncooperative twine. When that didn't work, he let his mind drift toward the smoky graveyard of his family, a treasure chest of the faded ghosts of his father, mother and only brother, Henry, who was two years younger but in the ground for going on six years now.

He could still hear their voices in his mind. They beckoned him on those bleak days in the valley, telling him to return to a home that was long gone. His father's laughter boomed as they ran together past the cattle, waiting for them to give chase. Tom heard his brother making gun-pop noises as he played with little green army men in the sand. But most of all he could hear his mother calling him for supper whenever the last bit of sunlight marbled the sky to velvet, her voice high and musical, the sound of instant trust. The memories of all of his dogs came with those voices, as if summoned by them, and sometimes he could almost see the shadows of their tails bobbing in the fields and feel their hot breath on the back of his hands.

Every day, Tom's age occurred to him in a way it never had when he'd been a younger man. He found himself confused by his own reflection and shocked by the calendar year. It was as if someone had snipped a large portion of his life away, like a film editor removes an unwanted scene. He knew now how time eroded, and while he wanted this bitter knowledge to give him an inner fire to savor life, instead all it did was remind him of the frailty of it, and of its ever-approaching expiration date.

If a little girl could die like that...

CHAPTER ELEVEN

"I think you should come down to the station."

The morning was frozen and mean and Tom hadn't even eaten breakfast yet.

"What's happened, Dale?"

"It's Reston."

"Y'all caught him?"

"Not exactly. He turned himself in last night."

Tom was taken aback. "Hell, I wouldna thought a man in his position would do such a thing."

"Ayuh, well, he claims he's innocent, of course. Says he was shocked to see his face on the news so he called the police."

"What'd he say to you?"

"Didn't call me. He was in Dayton County and called the local station."

"Dayton?"

"Yep. Looks like he took my get-out-of-town threat pretty serious."

Dayton County was a good six-hour drive from Coyote Valley. It was also west of it, the opposite direction from Boston, where Reston claimed to be from.

"What in hell was he doin out there?"

"Driftin, same as anywheres else he's been. But as it turns out he's got some friends in Gloucester, which is where he was staying."

"Even scum has buddies, huh?"

"And that's where we're gonna have some trouble, Tom."

"How's that?"

"These friends of his give him an alibi on the day the MacDougall girl was killed. And not just his friends, but some folks in a local bar too. He says they'll all tell us he was there in Gloucester when it happened."

Tom's breath escaped him.

"One other thing," Dale said. "Alice's body showed no signs of rape or molestation. No traces of semen. So the creep threatened it, according to Paige, but he didn't go through with that part. He just killed her and ran."

Tom had no words. His thoughts were scrambled now, static.

"There's still a lot to sort out," Dale said.

⤳

At the station, Dale told Tom he thought it was best that a professional interview Paige.

"Well," Tom said, "no offense, Dale, but ain't you and your boys professionals?"

"That's not what I mean. There are agencies that have special facilities and equipment for interviewin children."

"Equipment? What the hell do you mean by that?"

"Now, don't get excited, Tom. She's not gonna be hooked up to no electrodes or anythin. These are safe houses filled with children's furniture and toys. The interviewer is someone specifically trained in interviewin kids."

"But she already told you everythin."

"Welp, frankly, I should've done this in the first place. Interviewin a child, especially about a murder… the questionin itself can be traumatic. Fear will mess with a person's memory. Paige didn't shut down, but we still didn't really get what we needed. Some kids can be heavily influenced by an adult's questionin. They're too eager to please in most cases, just to get it over with, and it can change their own recollection of the incident. They can end up givin you false information without ever intendin to."

"And you think that's what happened when she talked with Cole?"

"Cole is a good detective, but I just want Paige to be able to give us her own complete version of what happened, missin no details, no matter how minor, and not havin her story accidentally altered."

Tom leaned back with a sigh. "Don't you think makin her go through this over and over again can traumatize her too? I worry about that, Dale. I worry about it a lot. I mean, all these interrogations—"

"Now hold on there, she's not bein *interrogated*, just questioned. In fact, I'm tryin to make this feel as little like an interrogation as possible. That's the whole point of bringin in a specialist."

Tom sat there silently, looking at his folded hands. He thought of Paige sitting out in the lobby, and wondered what she was truly feeling as her grandfather went behind closed doors with the police again.

"About the shrink lady…" Dale said. "How's that been goin?"

"Good, I guess. It's hard to tell one way or the other."

"Well, it can take time—"

"I want to be with her."

"Pardon?"

"When the specialist interviews Paige, I want to be there with her. I'm her guardian, I have a right, ain't I?"

"Of course. Tom, this is all up to you. I'm askin for you and Paige's help to solve a murder here, but I'm lookin out for y'all's best interest too. Bottom line is you're her grandpop. You're within your rights to ask that, and you're also within your rights to ask that she not be interviewed at all."

He let that sink in.

"I want to cooperate, Dale. So does Paige, you know that."

"Ayuh."

"When and where you wanna do this?"

"Soon as I get word, I'll let ya know. I'll set it all up and keep it as close to home as possible for ya."

"What about Reston?"

"He's cooperating right now, but he's also waitin on his lawyer to come in from Massachusetts before we get right down to it."

"Has he been charged?"

"Without a murder weapon or a clear motive, it'd be hard to make a charge stick. Especially if these alibis of his prove rock hard. I want to wait to arrest him because once we do we have limited time to take him to court for his arraignment, and the judge might decide he can be released on bail. As long as he's cooperatin like he is now, we can wait to slap him with the charge until we have a more solid case. And a clear, professionally gathered statement from Paige, our only eye witness, will help that."

Tom nodded. "How're the MacDougalls doin?"

"About like you'd expect."

"I haven't heard anythin about services yet."

"Reckon their grief is too heavy to deal with it all. Last I heard was the whole family has come in to help. I'm sure somethin will be announced soon."

Tom hung his head. "Shit, Dale. If I'd just kept the girls in my sight instead of lettin em go off into the woods—"

"Don't think like that, Tom. Ain't your fault what happened."

"I thought about maybe sendin the family something—food or flowers. I don't think I could handle stoppin by."

"I'd let it go for the time bein. Mrs. MacDougall is not in a good way. The best way you can help that family now is to help us get the whole truth from Paige, so we can make sure we nail who did this."

———

Because there was such an outpouring of condolences from all of Middlebury, an open wake was being held for Alice MacDougall on Monday with a private burial service for the family at an undisclosed date. There was a half-page announcement in the paper and folks were talking about it at The Blue Streak Diner in hushed tones. It was the first thing customers mentioned to Hannah Green when they sat down, even before looking at the menu. Russ wasn't interested in talking sports or politics, which was a first.

"I'm going to close the diner for it," he told Tom. "Everyone in town oughta pay their respects."

"Seems only right," Tom said.

Hannah came by with the coffee pot in her hand. "I'm just so glad the other girl is okay."

Tom was hearing this a lot, and was beginning to wonder if Paige's identity had been revealed. Throughout the diner gossip stirred, not just about the MacDougalls and the wake, but also the man being held by the police, Jason Reston. Tom heard more than one person mention the "good ol' days" when all that was needed was a rope and a high tree to dish out justice. Tom dropped off Russ's most recent order of cuts and ground beef and left without having breakfast.

At the feed store, Ed asked how the new pump was working out for him, but like everyone else he seemed on the verge of asking about the murder. Tom had been back and forth to the police station with Paige. Someone must have noticed and spread the word... unless the MacDougalls had released the information, though Tom doubted they would have done something so foolish. If Tom's suspicion was correct, everyone would have put it together that Paige was the one who had been with Alice when she died. Thankfully, like everyone else, Ed respectfully resisted the temptation to pry.

He had done the right thing by keeping Paige out of school. If adults had this much trouble dealing with the news, he could only imagine how children were going to react. But Paige wanted to go back. She'd told him that flat out, so they came to an agreement to wait until after the wake.

Perhaps the catharsis of the services would help cleanse the townspeople of some of the darkness that had been encircling them these past few days. He believed it would calm things down, at least a little bit. Dr. White told him it would be good for Paige to get back to her normal routine so she could get on with her life at her own pace. She saw it as a good sign that the girl was interested in returning to school, and Tom figured she knew better than he did, being the professional and all. Hopefully she was right. He certainly wanted to believe she was.

When he arrived at Downtown Market it was nearing eleven in the morning. Only a few patrons wandered the aisles and even less were sitting in the lounge by the coffee bar. The store was Middlebury's attempt to have a combination indoor farmer's market, local brewery, artisan coffee shop, and fancy all-natural deli. It appealed to the sense of supporting local and eating fresh—prevalent in Vermont—and reflected the trendy downtown districts of bigger cities, only on a much smaller scale. Tom's beef and chicken was sold at the meat counter, which also sold other local meats and fish, some fresh and some frozen. It was his most profitable partnership.

Jeff Summerson was wiping down the glass case when Tom approached, hauling one of his foam coolers. Jeff gave him his crooked smile. The men shook hands.

"Back from the slaughtahouse already, huh?" Jeff asked, his thick New England accent ringing.

"They work fast now that they've expanded."

"Hear one's goin up that's gonna be closah."

"That'd be nice. Guess we'll see."

Tom looked up at the hand-drawn chalk art signs that hung above the counter, advertising all of the local farms that were represented by the market. He was delighted to see one for his own, Lone Valley Ranch, with a big bull's head underneath the name.

"Great artwork," he said.

"Ayuh. Mah niece does em for us. Kid's got a talent. Just hope the ownah likes em."

"Well, I sure like mine."

"I don't mean you ranchas and fahmas. I mean the ownah of this here grocery mahket. They'll be in town this weekend, for the big funeral."

"Oh." Tom raised his eyebrows. "That's interesting."

"Not really."

"What do you mean?"

"Gerald Sands is the head of the company that owns this place.

His sista is the mama of that lil girl done got killed."

"You mean he's Alice MacDougall's uncle?"

"You put that together, did ya?" His paper hat slid on his grayed head as he stood upright. "You're a quick one, Tommy."

Tom had been working with Downtown Market for three years now and had never known that Fay MacDougall had a relation to the head of Fresh Food Corp, the parent company. He'd never dealt with Sands or heard much about him, always dealing with the market on its base level.

"I just wasn't aware of that," he said.

"Ayuh. The Sands family must own halfa this town at this point." Jeff took a deep breath, his thoughts visibly wandering. "Damned shame about their loss. Damned shame. I understan him wantin to check on the mahket while he's in town, but I'm sure surprised Sands could have a mind for business at a time like this."

CHAPTER TWELVE

They ate lunch at the table, but once again Paige was picking at her food more than eating it.

"You feelin okay about bein talked to tomorrow?" Tom asked.

She spoke to her food, twirling it at the end of her fork and then diving it back down onto the plate. "I guess so."

Her face was slate. She seemed not just lost in herself, but entombed.

"Just tell em everythin that happened. Every little detail. That way they can put this fella behind bars where he belongs. Okay?"

"Okay."

Tom's shoulders sagged and he put down his fork. "Paige, I want you to look at me."

It took a moment, then the hoods of her eyes came up, revealing the deep, brown beneath, but only for a quick flash. He waited and her gaze returned, and this time she held it.

"It's gonna be all right, honey," he said, putting his hand over hers. "It's all gonna be all right. All we gotta do is get through this one thing, and then we can put it all behind us. I know this has been hard on you. You've been through so much for a girl your age. And you've been brave."

This got a small smile out of her.

"I just want you to know that I understand," Tom said, hoping to connect. "And I'm proud of you."

Her gazed lowered again, but she nodded. He hoped he had comforted her, but couldn't know for sure. It wouldn't do their relationship any good to press it. Tom knew from experience with people as well as animals that relationships move in stages. There was a robotic stage at first where you just tried to make things work and see if all the parts fit, and then there was a motivational stage where you discovered what made the other happy and why they were special, and used that to form a connection. Only after achieving these stages could you advance to a stage of spirituality and pure love. That was the relationship stage that made marriages, bonded families, shaped horses, and turned dogs into best friends. With Paige, these stages seemed not only to take longer but also to relapse again and again, so that their relationship was always moving forward and then falling back, leaving them in an emotional purgatory.

"You think her funeral will be nice?" she asked.

"Well, what we'll be at is a wake. But I think it will be very nice, yes."

"I think so too. She always had nice things."

Tom nodded, chewing.

"What's the difference?" Paige asked.

"Between what?"

"A funeral and a wake."

"A wake is when everybody can sort of come together and talk about the departed. A funeral is when they get buried."

"So the wake is like a party?"

"Well, it ain't festive. It's more like a get-together to celebrate the memory of the person who's died."

"A celebration?"

"Yeah."

She went back to picking at her food. Tom thought back to the funeral of the girl's parents. Because of the mangled condition of the bodies, he'd passed on the idea of having a wake. He hoped Paige wouldn't resent this.

"You think you wanna say a few words at the wake?" he asked.

She kept picking.

"You were her best friend. Might be nice, if you feel up to it. No one's gonna make you. Just a thought is all."

"What would I say?"

"Oh, you know, just talk about her, what she was like, what she meant to you. Talk about the games you used to play—"

"Games?" Her face went hard, her eyes glaring. "What do you mean *games*?"

Tom blinked. "I just meant what y'all played."

She scooted back her chair. "No! That's our world. Ours. Nobody else's."

"Well, honey, you don't have to talk about that then."

"I can't. It's forbidden. Not that I'd want to."

Tom leaned forward, his brow furrowed. "Forbidden?"

"You wouldn't understand. Only Alice and I do."

He noticed how she was speaking about the girl in the present tense. "Alright, Paige. I know what you and Alice had was special. That's yours to keep."

She held his gaze for a moment, her frown never fading, and then went right back to picking at her food, most of which would end up getting fed to Jep who lay beneath the table, waiting for next morsel to drop.

CHAPTER THIRTEEN

Tom watched the interviewer establish a rapport. The woman introduced herself as Emma Rowe and began by asking Paige about things that had nothing to do with the murder—the girl's daily life, what her favorite hobbies were, what subjects she liked in school, what TV shows and movies were her favorites. Tom wished he'd been able to talk this easily with Paige. Rowe was a young child psychologist, pleasant and approachable, as well as very good at her job, from what Tom was seeing.

"We don't want to interview her about this too many times," she'd told him in private. "Not only will that stress her but it will get her too used to repeating the same old answers, so then when she goes on the stand her testimony will seem rehearsed."

Tom hated the idea of Paige being put before a courtroom, berated by attorneys and judged by a jury comprised of their neighbors, her classmates' parents.

"I have the recording of Sergeant Cole's interview," Rowe had explained. "I just want to clarify any ambiguities in her account. I'll be using all open-ended questions this first session."

And that's what she was doing now, and Tom was pleasantly surprised by her success. Paige was opening up more than he'd ever seen her do with anyone. She played with the Legos on the coffee table and kicked her legs in her seat.

"If I had to pick one, I think soccer is my favorite sport."

Rowe offered a motherly smile. "How come?"

"I like using my feet instead of my hands."

They talked like this for some time, Tom sitting silent, happy when Paige held his hand but happier when she got comfortable enough to let go. Only when Paige seemed at her most at ease with Rowe did the interview start to turn toward the murder, slowly and cautiously, allowing Paige to tell it her own way.

"We always played in the woods, so that's what we were doing."

"And what happened on this particular day?"

Paige looked away and stopped playing with the toys.

"It's okay," Rowe said. "Just take it a little at a time."

"We were playing like we always do."

"What did you two like to play?"

"Just stuff," Paige said, her upper body going tense.

"Okay. What happened then?"

"I saw him in the bushes."

"What was he doing?"

"Watching us play. He was hiding, but I saw him. And he saw me looking at him."

"And what happened then?"

Paige's voice dropped an octave and she looked at her sneakers. She reached for a stuffed bear on the sofa and began to pluck at its fur. "He came out of the bushes and grabbed Alice."

"I know this is hard, but tell me what he did when he grabbed her, Paige. I need to know."

Paige's face lost color. Tom almost reached for her hand but decided against it. He didn't want to interrupt.

"You know what he did," Paige said.

"We just need to go over it."

"I already told the other cop."

"I know. But I'd really appreciate it if you told it to me."

Paige grimaced. "He had a knife. He started stabbing her."

"What kind of knife did he have? Could you see?"

"A big kitchen knife."

"Did he say anything?"

"No."

"And what did you do?"

"I screamed and ran away so he wouldn't get me too."

Tom expected to hear a quiver in her voice and see a swelling in her eyes, but the child remained stoic. It upset him far more.

"I have a hard question for you now, Paige, but it's important and I know you're a strong girl, so here goes. What was the last thing you saw before you ran away?"

It took her a moment before she spoke. "He was stabbing her and she was screaming and bleeding."

"How was he stabbing her? Was he raising his arm up like this?" She raised her hand above her head. "Or like this?" She lowered her arm and turned her palm face up.

"The second one."

"Can you tell me where on her body?"

Another pause, eyes downcast. "Her belly."

"Did you see him do anything else?"

"No."

"What did he do with the knife?"

57

"What do you mean?"

"Did he drop it somewhere or do anything else with it?"

"No."

"Okay. What kind of things did he say to you and Alice?"

Paige looked to her grandfather, a fresh nervousness twitching in her face. He placed his hand on her back.

"It's okay," Rowe said. "You can tell us."

"He said dirty things."

"Like what?"

She glanced at Tom. "They're bad words."

"You can say them, honey," Tom said. "It's all right to here. Just to help catch him."

She dropped her head again, her face going pink. "He said he was gonna fuck us. He said he was gonna fuck our little pussies and kill us."

Heaviness filled the room like fog. Tom grit his teeth and struggled not to show it. Rowe, ever the professional, kept an even tone and her warm expression didn't falter.

"What else did he say?"

"Just that. That's all."

There was a pause, the vents above whispering heat.

"Did you or Alice know this man?" Rowe asked.

"No. He was a stranger."

"Had you ever seen him before?"

"Yeah, when he was in our yard. My grandpa went outside with his gun and told him to get lost."

Rowe smirked at Tom. He tried not to blush and she returned her attention to Paige.

"So you're sure it was the same man then?"

Paige nodded.

"Can I show you a few pictures?"

"Okay."

Rowe took a folder from the table and withdrew several glossy prints. There were ten pictures of six different men, some mug shots and some regular shots. Two of them were clearly Reston, one his most recent mug shot from when he turned himself in, the other was of him leaning against a brick building.

"Just point to the man that attacked you. The one that hurt Alice."

Paige reached out and put a hand on the picture of Reston leaning on the wall.

"Okay. Now can you pick out his face?"

Paige took a moment to look them over, and then selected one of the mug shots.

It was not the one of Reston.

"Are you sure that's him?"

"Yeah."

"Do you want to look at the pictures a little more?"

"No, that's him. I said I'm sure."

"Okay. Thank you, Paige, for everything you've helped me with."

Paige sighed. "Yeah, okay."

"What else can you tell me about that day?"

"Nothing. I just ran and got my grandpa."

"Well, that was the right thing to do."

They talked some more and Rowe slowly drew the conversation back to more pleasant things, speaking with the child the way she had at the beginning, talking about cartoons and toys. Rowe then asked Paige to go with another woman to the rec room so she could play video games and have a snack while Rowe spoke with her grandpa.

"She gets very wooden talking about it," Rowe told him. "She never cries or even chokes up. I think she's desensitized herself to protect herself. The memories are too vicious for her to face them emotionally."

"She was like that when her mom and dad died too. I think it might just be her way."

"It's a coping mechanism more common to adults. Unusual for a girl her age."

"Well, she's got a good shrink now." He hoped he hadn't offended her with the term. "I mean, a psychiatrist. A nice lady like you."

"That's good. It's also good that the story she told me today is consistent with the one she told Cole, but she gave me a few more small details. I think she's more comfortable with a woman. Our one problem is that she picked out the right photo at first but then picked the wrong mug shot."

"But that one she picked still sorta looked like Reston."

"It did, but it wasn't him. Plus that guy had thinning hair and a moustache. Reston doesn't. Sheriff Rogers will want to do a lineup. That'll be best."

Tom groaned at the idea of putting Paige through more of this. "Christ. I don't want her to have to see that man face to face again. She'll be terrified."

"It's two-way glass. He won't see her."

"I know, but she'll still have to see him in the flesh, and she's a kid. She might not trust us when we tell her he can't see in."

"These things are never easy, especially with a child. But I think she'll trust you. If we drive home that we're trying to put this man in jail so he will never hurt anyone again, it can give her more motivation, more courage."

Tom saw genuine empathy in the woman's eyes. There was a softness to her, a yielding he would have been drawn to as a younger man.

"Well," he said. "Is that it?"

"For today. One quick question though. She locked up on me when I asked her what they were playing. Do you know why that is?"

"They had some sort of special game between just the two of them, one of those best friend things that no one else gets to know about. You know little girls and their secrets."

Rowe gave him a knowing smile. "I'm afraid I do, Mr. Hargrave. I'm afraid I do."

CHAPTER FOURTEEN

The sun broke through on the day of the wake. At the start it was just a hole in the sky hiding behind a haze, but by the time they arrived at the funeral hall the clouds had given way to a brilliant blue. The sun's warmth made it the most tolerable one in weeks.

The turnout was even bigger than expected. Main Street had to be closed off for the procession, and the funeral home opted to open their hall to have enough space for all the bereaved. It seemed as if the whole town shut down to attend the services. Tom saw his neighbors Fred Hollister and his son Willard. He saw the Godfreys, and the two boys waved to him just like they always did at the bus stop. Russ Redburn had been true to his word and closed the diner, and he was there with Ed and Hannah Green, who was dabbing her eyes with a handkerchief. Tom almost didn't recognize Jeff Summerson without his paper hat and bloody apron. He saw a lot of faces he recognized from around town, some he hadn't seen in years. There were unfamiliar faces too, and he wondered how many people had come from out of town.

Sheriff Dale Rogers, Officer Cooper Struve and Detective Deontay Cole arrived in suits. Several other uniformed officers were there to direct traffic. Tom respected Dale for coming but worried that if by doing so he was opening himself up to criticism from the grief-stricken for not solving the case yet.

Inside the hall it was stuffy and smelled of artificial lilac. Tom was glad he'd left his overcoat in the truck. His only suit had been purchased a long time ago and the pants were a lot tighter now. The coat pinched his armpits. He wasn't able to get his shirt buttoned at the neck so he'd tied a high knot on his tie to cover it up. He broke out his black Stetson for the affair, the one Betty had bought him for special occasions. "This one's not for wrangling cattle in the mud," she had told him. "It's for weddings and graduations and the like." Not many people in Vermont wore cowboy hats to formal occasions, but Tom was old-fashioned that way and refused to change.

Paige had put on her dark blue dress; the same one she'd worn at her parents' funeral. He'd had it cleaned and pressed for her. In her hair were little white ribbons and her shoes gleamed like marbles.

In a tiny coffin at the head of the first room lay Alice MacDougall.

The coffin was open just enough to see her face and shoulders. She was wearing rouge, the mortician having powdered her up to make her look alive. Tom had read somewhere that they glued the eyelids shut and put toothpicks in their lips to keep them closed. He tried to push the thought away.

Beside the coffin stood the MacDougalls and their extended family, shaking hands with those in attendance as they walked up to pay their respects. Tom recognized Fay's husband, Troy MacDougall, from the few times he took Alice to and from the bus stop. The man looked as if he'd lost ten pounds since he'd last seen him, a twig threatening to break at the slightest breeze. His cheeks were sunken, the flesh of his neck hanging down like that of an older man, and his eyes were buried within the purpled caves of his skull.

Fay was dressed immaculately in black, weeping openly beneath the veil of her hat. She leaned on her husband, her words slurring. Tom felt embarrassed for her, but he also couldn't blame her. In her shoes, he would have been drunk too. After Betty died, he'd almost gone back to bourbon to souse his grief, but decided it was better to keep the promise he'd made his wife ten years ago, when she'd finally threatened to leave if he didn't get sober. He'd worked too hard to let her down now.

Tom guided Paige behind Ed and Hannah in the growing line. The couple turned to them.

"Good of y'all to come out," Tom said.

Ed shook Tom's hand. "Wouldn't miss it. Somethin like this… Hell. It affects all of us."

Beside him Hannah breathed heavily, tears running unashamed.

"Just a baby," she kept repeating.

"Sands is here, by the way," Ed told him.

Tom wasn't sure what he meant by that. "Okay."

"Gerald Sands." Ed pointed nonchalantly.

Tom saw a tall, strapping man standing beside the MacDougalls. He looked to be in his mid-thirties, with close-shaved hair that accentuated his strong features, and there was an intimidating iciness to him, the kind of stoic grimace a corporate man carries like a badge. He seemed to be staring at everyone and no one all at once.

"His company's got a claim in most of the businesses in this here town," Ed said. "Being their VP, he practically owns the Downtown Market, and he has his own ventures too. We rent the property from him for our store. He's not why we're here, but it's a good idea to pay respects to him, Tom. Let him know you were here, know what

I mean?"

Tom nodded. As much as both men hated to think about it right now, there was no bad time to network, even if it just meant showing your face. A small businessman needed all the help he could get.

As they approached the casket, Ed and Hannah took a moment to gaze upon Alice. The MacDougalls noticed Tom and Paige behind them.

Troy locked eyes with Tom for a moment then turned to Paige and smiled. "Hey there, kiddo."

Though he barely knew either of them, Tom had always liked Troy more than Fay. He was far humbler, making him more approachable than his wife. Paige gave him a weak smile and he got on one knee and took her hand.

"Thank you for coming, sweetheart. Alice always told me you were her best friend. She loved you like a sister."

His arm went around her and he drew Paige in. Tom thought she was a little uncomfortable, but she didn't resist the embrace. Fay hovered above them, her eyes on Paige. The look on her face was one of nauseous unhappiness, contorted by a grief no mother should ever know.

"It's not fair..." she muttered.

Her husband looked back at her. "Fay..."

"Don't you fucking *Fay* me. It's not... fucking... *fair*, Troy. None of this is *fucking fair*!"

Her fists clenched at her sides, teeth flashing like razors.

"Mrs. MacDougall, please," Tom said.

"Don't you tell me what to do! You don't know me. You don't know my pain. She's alive and my Alice is dead. Dead!" She pointed at Paige who had frozen like a cornered cat. "Look at her! She's not crying or anything. She doesn't care. I always knew there was something weird about her!"

Troy went to his wife and took her in his arms, trying to move her away. Fay shook loose from him, losing her balance in the process, and fell against the casket, rocking it and nearly pushing it over. She tried to stand and fell into Ed Green, who caught her under her armpits as she went limp. The crowd gasped at the spectacle, many looking away, embarrassed for the grieving woman.

Troy's eyes were wet. "I'm so sorry."

"It's all right," Tom said.

It wasn't, but Fay was drunk and hysterical. Even so, he was shocked by how she had lashed out at Paige. She was only ten years old for Christ's sake, and she'd been Alice's closest friend. Her own father had just said so.

Thinking it was best to move on, Tom put his hands on Paige's shoulders. He'd wanted her to be able to say a final goodbye to Alice, but given the circumstances he chose to take her as far away from Fay MacDougall as possible. Besides, the last thing a little girl needed was to see a dead body and feel how cold it was. Tom would never forget when he kissed his mother goodbye on her forehead as she lay in her coffin before him, and how it had felt like he was kissing a glacier. This wake had been bad enough without adding something like that to it.

Moving along, he shook hands with the rest of the family, none of which he knew, each of them apologetic about Fay. They beamed at Paige, as if her sheer youth was enough to give them hope in this dark chapter of their lives.

'She's so beautiful," a woman said.

"A real sweetheart," said another.

Paige maintained a shy silence. When at last they reached Gerald Sands, Tom put out his hand. Sands slightly hesitated before shaking it.

"Tom Hargrave," Tom said.

"Gerald Sands. I'm Fay's brother."

The man was detached, robotic.

"A pleasure. My condolences to you."

"I hope you'll forgive my sister. She is overwhelmed right now."

"Understandably so. It's all right."

Sands rolled his shoulders beneath an expensive-looking suit. "I'm glad you came, Mr. Hargrave. And little Paige too. I was wondering if I could speak to you a moment, away from all of this."

"Sure, all right."

"It's too crowded in here, let's go outside."

Tom tilted his head. "You mean, right now?"

"Certainly. It won't take long."

Sands started walking and Tom followed after him. He thought about leaving Paige inside but decided against it given all that had just happened. He wasn't sure what Sands wanted, but Tom was ready to leave anyhow.

Outside the cold was rich and dry. Abundant sunshine made the piles of snow blinding. Even more cars were funneling in and there was frustrated energy as they searched for parking. Tom walked Paige to the truck and told her he'd be right back. She pulled her stuffed tiger from the seat and held it in her lap, making its paws move around. Tom went back to Sands and they walked to the side of the building to hide from the bite of the wind.

"What can I help ya with?" Tom asked.

"Mr. Hargrave, I'd just like to ask you about what happened."

Tom tensed. "Pardon me?"

"The day of the murder. You found the body, and your granddaughter saw everything. Isn't that right?"

"It is."

"Now, I certainly understand you wanting to keep this clandestine. But I'm family, and I'm no happier with the way this sordid investigation has gone than my poor sister is."

"Sheriff Rogers has the man. It's just a matter of makin a rock-hard case."

"That's exactly my point. Maybe there's something more out there that he could use. More concrete information."

Tom cleared his throat, irked by Sand's implications. "Sir?"

"I know your granddaughter's just a girl. But maybe she's withholding something, perhaps without even realizing it. I think it would beneficial for all parties concerned if Paige was talked to more thoroughly. I've decided to hire an investigator of my own, and my attorney is—"

"Hold on just a minute now. Paige has already been interviewed by the police and a specialist. She ain't keepin nothing back. Now, this whole thing has been hard on her and havin her interrogated again and again can be traumatic."

"Interrogated?"

Tom blinked. "Yeah."

"Interesting choice of words, Mr. Hargrave."

Tom felt something turn inside of him, flushing him in a sour way.

"I'm not sure what you're tryin to say, Mr. Sands."

"Just that we think there is more to unveil, and that we're hoping you'll be cooperative."

He put out his hand, and this time it was Tom who hesitated before shaking it.

"We'll be in touch, Mr. Hargrave. But for now, I need to return to the wake, and tend to my poor, crestfallen little sister."

CHAPTER FIFTEEN

The lineup didn't take long. Behind the glass, the four men stepped forward and said the words.

"I'm gonna fuck your little pussies and kill you."

Each time, Tom winced and Dale appeared just as uncomfortable with Paige there. After the men in the lineup had done their bit, they all stepped forward together and Dale asked Paige to pick out the man that had killed Alice.

Paige was quick to decide.

"Him," she said, pointing.

The man she chose was neither Reston nor the man she'd chosen from the mug shot.

CHAPTER SIXTEEN

"The district attorney doesn't think we have enough," Dale said.

Tom was riding Essie away from the smaller quarantine barn where his new bred-back cow/calf combinations were being kept. Because they were a more productive unit they'd been more expensive, but he was excited about the quicker income stream. He'd spent the morning considering surface drainage patterns and the prevailing winds while checking valves and tightening up the bumper gate. His hands ached from working the cold metal, and he fumbled now while trying to keep the cell phone to his ear.

"She thinks there ain't no case against Reston," Dale said.

"Jesus, Dale."

"Well, I can see where she's comin from. Reston has solid alibis and receipts from a motel he checked into in Dayton. We have no murder weapon and the one witness failed to identify him. On top of this, Reston has no violent priors or sex offenses."

Tom sagged in the saddle, not sure what to say. He also understood where the district attorney was coming from, and nobody wanted to see an innocent man go to jail, but it pained him to think that the guilty would go free.

"Tom, unless there is anythin else you or Paige can remember, we're kinda at a standstill here."

"Sands seems to think there's somethin more."

"I'm sorry?"

"Gerald Sands. Alice's uncle."

"Oh, I know who he is, but what about him?"

"He approached me at the funeral. Says he has an attorney and a private eye or somethin. Says he wants to look more into the case. He thinks maybe Paige isn't tellin us everythin about what happened."

The sheriff grumbled. "Aw, Christ."

"Says he hopes we'll cooperate."

"This guy is a real hard ass, Tom. Comes from money and isn't afraid to throw it around. But this is a police matter. You don't have to talk to him or his people."

"You gonna tell him to back off?"

"Why? He seem aggressive?"

"No, but I don't want Paige gettin pressured. She's been through enough as it is."

"Well, I can't stop him from hirin a private investigator. I'm sure you can get them to be reasonable when it comes to Paige. Just keep me in the loop."

"Ayuh. I will. So you're gonna let Reston go then?"

"It's lookin that way."

Tom looked to the sky. "Jesus, Mary and Joseph."

"If we arrest him now with nothin to go on, we're just gonna fail. If we wait to find solid evidence against him or someone else, we'll be better off for it."

"And what if he is the killer and he comes back here to finish what he started? What if he comes for my granddaughter?"

Dale was hushed. "Like I said the other day, you're within your rights to protect yourself. But don't worry. Reston will be here in town for a while because we want him to be. And he's gonna be watched and watched close."

"So what happens now?"

"We're workin on it. There'll be another full sweep of the woods, so you'll be seein us around. Until then, let me know if anythin comes up or if either of you remember somethin new."

It was a bleak afternoon. The lifeless sugar maples loomed, spotted by browned, wet moss, looking like twisted skeletons of their former selves. The lowland was as slushy as a mire, the snow having melted and refrozen, creating dangerous ground. Tom worried Paige might slip as she came off the bus. Once inside the truck, she slammed the door behind her. Tom stared at her, noting the fury in her eyes.

"What's a matter, darlin?"

"Stupid kids at school! I hate them!"

"What happened?"

"I wanna go home!"

"Okay, we're goin, we're goin." He put the truck in gear and the tires crunched the black snow of the shoulder. "You wanna tell me what's going on?"

"No!"

"Watch your tone, young lady." He'd been letting things slide given all she'd been through, but she was starting to test him. "Now if some kid is hasslin you at school, you tell me and we'll fix it."

"It's not just some kid, Grandpa. It's a whole bunch of em!

They're teasing me. Bobby Williams was making stabbing motions with his pen, saying 'I'm gonna get you, Paige!' And everybody laughed!"

Tom's hands clenched the wheel, his knuckles becoming ghosts.

"I hope you socked him one," he said.

"I wanted to stomp on his foot!"

"Did ya?"

"No." Paige pouted her lips. "Everyone was laughing at me. They think what happened is funny."

"It can't be everyone."

"Well, there was five of em; Jessie, Mandy, Dakota, and Lyle, and some other girl. They kept saying the boogeyman was gonna come back for me." Her eyes burned and she began to breath heavily. "They're saying that… the boogeyman…"

"Hey now, nobody's gonna get you, darlin." He put an arm around her and drew her near. "Those kids are just bein lil brats. You tell em to go screw."

She snickered despite how upset she was.

"You tell your teacher about them lil jerks?"

"No. Then the other kids would just make fun of me even more."

"Maybe so. Maybe so. But you don't have to take that crap. You know, when I was a younger man, I did a little boxin. Maybe we oughta go to the ol' gym and I can teach ya how to hit the heavy bag. Next time that Bobby opens his mouth you can fustigate him."

"What's fustigate?"

"My old man used to say that all the time. It means *kick some butt*."

"But Bobby's a boy."

"All the better. He'll be extra ashamed to get his ass whooped by a girl."

She laughed again and the sound filled him with fresh hope.

"I'd love to knock his block off," she admitted.

"Well, you want your old grandpa to teach you how to stick and move?"

"You want me to hit him with a stick?"

Now it was Tom who laughed.

~✕~

Tom noticed the Lincoln Town Car parked outside their home as they pulled into the driveway. The car was running, and there was a man

69

sitting inside. Tom's Marlin 336 hunting rifle was in the truck's cabin and he reached for it after putting the truck in park.

There was a tremor in Paige's voice. "Who's that, Grandpa?"

"Don't know. Just stay in the truck, darlin."

Before Tom could get out, the Town Car shut off and a stout man with silvery hair stepped out. He was close to Tom's age, well dressed beneath a long overcoat. He waved with one hand. Tom's fear subsided so he released his grip on the rifle and stepped down from the truck. There was a gentle dusting in the air, snowflakes swirling like confetti. Tom approached the man gingerly, keeping his distance. The man however, walked briskly, his hand out.

"Mr. Hargrave, I presume?"

Tom nodded. "Who might you be?"

"I'm Martin Donati. I'm an investigator."

They shook hands.

"Police?"

"No, I'm a private investigator. I was hired by Gerald Sands to investigate the murder of his niece, Alice MacDougall. I was hoping I could talk to you and your granddaughter."

"You always show up unannounced like this?"

"I'm sorry, is this a bad time?"

"Paige is just now gettin home from school. Besides, she didn't have a very good day."

"I'm sorry to hear that."

"Well, truth is she's had a lot of bad days since this happened."

"So have the MacDougall's, Mr. Hargrave."

"I know, my heart goes out to em, but—"

"They know they have your condolences, and they assured me you'd want to help in any way you could."

This one's slicker than owl shit, Tom thought.

"Like I said, my heart goes out to them, but Paige has been through a lot too, Mr. Donati, and she's been interviewed about it all already. Makin her go over it again and again ain't gonna help matters, and it might just traumatize her if we force her. I'm sure the MacDougalls can understand that, and Mr. Sands too."

Donati smiled but his eyes were as blank as a granite slab. "Certainly no one wants to upset the child. But there is a murderer on the loose. Alice's family deserves to see him caught and tried. They deserve justice."

"No argument there."

"But to get that justice they need cooperation. Paige's

cooperation, specifically. We need her to be upfront, collegial."

Behind him, Tom heard the door to the truck opening. He turned to see Paige step down and shut the door behind her. She didn't move forward, watching the men with hard, dark eyes. The small bit of joy he'd managed to rise out of her moments ago had been extinguished. She was back to her silent, morose self, and that made Tom even angrier with Donati, and Gerald Sands too.

"Hello, sweetheart," Donati said, waving.

"We need to go inside now," Tom said.

"Good, good. Thank you, I appreciate that."

"That wasn't an invitation. I meant my granddaughter and I have to go inside."

He went to Paige and took her arm. They started walking past Donati but he stepped in front of them, his hands up passively but blocking their path nonetheless.

"Please," he said, still smiling as if they were old friends. "Just give me a little time, that's all. Just a few questions and I'll be out of your hair."

"It's time for you to leave, mister. Now step side."

"Be reasonable, Hargrave. Your granddaughter's the only witness."

Tom felt his last nerve sever as a mean heat rose up his chest.

"You gonna move?" he asked. "Or you want me to move you?"

Donati's smile turned smug, almost challenging. He stepped aside. Tom and Paige made their way to the porch as the snowflakes thickened, carried by a wind that was growing meaner, a threatening whisper of things to come.

"I'll be in touch," Donati said.

Tom ushered Paige inside. "Stay off of my property, Donati."

As Tom closed the door, the detective got one more word in.

"Have it your way, Hargrave."

CHAPTER SEVENTEEN

The backlash began the very next day and only got worse as the week went on. Tom lost sleep the night of Donati's visit, knowing that pushing back against Sands could hurt future prospects. He remembered something his brother Henry used to say: *Be careful of the toes you step on today because they might be connected to the ass you have to kiss tomorrow.*

It was a lesson Tom had learned the hard way, like most of the lessons he'd learned in life. If word got out that he was hindering any kind of investigation into the MacDougall case, it would make him a rather unpopular man in this town. It could hurt his reputation and even destroy his business. But he just couldn't let them press Paige. She'd been through more than enough as it was.

"Why does everyone want me to tell them the same things over and over?" she asked at dinner.

"Well, darlin, I guess that when people want an answer bad enough, they'll keep askin the same question until they get it, whether it's the right answer or not."

"I don't understand. What do they want me to say?"

"Don't worry about what they want. You already told the truth. That's all that matters."

Tom didn't stop at the diner on his way into town. He'd eaten a big breakfast when he'd gotten up early to tend to the livestock. He'd just been tossing and turning anyway.

The roads were still mushy out in the country, the plows having not made it out his way yet, but in the center of town the roads were cleared and heaps of snow made large rows beside the sidewalks. Tom pulled into the lot of Downtown Market.

When Jeff saw him enter, his face went slack and gaunt. Instead of looking at Tom when he approached, the butcher began fussing with the trays of meat from behind the counter—trays Tom saw were already full and packed with fresh ice because the market had just opened. Tom read bad news in the man's body language.

"Mornin, Jeff."

"Tom." The butcher glanced up.

"Came round to take a lil inventory and get your next order ready."

Jeff didn't reply. His shoulders sagged like burdened satchels. Tom came right up to the counter now and put his arms over top of it.

"They ain't told ya, have they?" Jeff asked.

"Afraid not. Guess that woulda been too decent."

"I'm sorry, Tom. Really."

"Wasn't your decision, I'm sure."

"Damn well wasn't. If I made them big decisions I wouldn't be standin behind this here counta."

"So no orderin from Tom Hargrave for the time bein?" Tom asked, trying to stay hopeful.

"No orderin from Tom Hargrave, period. Lone Valley Ranch is no longa a pahtna with Downtown Mahket."

Tom froze, noticing that the sign for his ranch had been taken down. A large portion of his income had been stripped away from him, just like that.

"They severed my partnership?"

"I'm sorry, Tom, real sorry. I can't believe they didn't at least tell ya themselves."

"Did Sands tell you this when he came in?"

"Nah. Word came down the corporate ladda, like these things do. I got the order in an email."

"But it was his decision."

"Ayuh, probably."

"Definitely." Tom banged his fist on the counter. "Shit!"

"Damn well stinks like it."

><

The hit Tom took at the market was a heavy one, but it hadn't totally blindsided him the way the one he got at Ed's feed store did. He went in for a few stakes and some alfalfa, but instead he came out with nothing but more worries.

"I'm sorry," Ed told him, "but I can't afford to have you coming in here."

"What the hell is this, Ed? I've been comin in here since you opened the place, and now you're givin me the shaft?"

"It's nothin personal. You know that."

"I just don't understand this. Sands is your landlord, but this is *your* business. He can't tell you who to sell to. What the hell did he say to you?"

"Nothin."

"Nothin?"

"It was that P.I., Donati. He came in here yesterday afternoon. Said he'd just went to see you. He was asking questions and saying that you weren't cooperating with him. Told me that it wouldn't sit well with Mr. Sands."

"So he told you not to do business with me? He can't do that, Ed!"

"Well, he didn't say it like that."

"How the hell did he say it then?"

"He kept, you know, *insinuating* things. Like telling me how bad for business it was when people don't cooperate. Asking me if I knew what he meant. Well, I do. I know what he means and I know what Sands means. He may just be my landlord, but my lease is up at the end of March. If I piss him off he might toss me or jack my rent to the sky, and then where would I be? His company owns half of Middlebury, Tom! I'd be shit out of luck and jolly well fucked."

Tom took a step back and looked down at his boots. They were as worn and faded as he felt. "How's he even gonna know I'm comin in here?"

"You know how people talk in small towns. I'm sorry, Tom, but I just can't risk it. I've gotta put my family first. I'm sure you can understand that."

Tom started toward the door. "I understand that just fine."

Tom still had the auction and video markets to sell his cattle, and he had orders from the diner and other restaurants for cuts and ground beef, and there were always the county farmer's markets when the weather changed. Still, he would need to do more promoting, something he'd gotten lazy with, especially after he'd let his business manager go to cut back on expenses. It was a decision he'd grown to regret. He could dip into his savings if he had to, but a new financial plan would have to be put in place to make up for lost sales.

He could get supplies from out of town, but the sting of being cut off from the immediate community burrowed deep, and Tom worried about what other screws Sands might be able to turn or could have turned already without Tom knowing about it. As children will turn their backs on the unpopular kid, many of Tom's friends would now turn their backs on him, lured away by the schoolyard bully, Gerald Sands.

At least ol' Jep won't ever betray me.

The dog trotted alongside Tom as he loped the ring of the ranch, looking for flaws. Jep dipped in and out of the piles of dead leaves that had been bunched toward the thicket in October, bobbing in and out of them, leaping in a sea of decay.

Though the sun beamed, the wind packed a bitter chill, and looking at the clear blue above, Tom felt a twinge of homesickness for Oklahoma and its big sky that reached out beyond the world and lapped right back over like a baby blanket. They had sunshine to spare out there. In the summertime it would turn Tom's neck as red and wet as lava, peeling away layers of flesh on his forehead and nose if he forgot his cowboy hat. His boots would pool with sweat while riding, clothes clinging to him. He'd always liked the move up north because it got him away from that vicious heat, but these Vermont winters sometimes made him regret it, especially now that he was getting old.

When he got back to the house he took a bath to warm up his bones. The arthritis in his knuckles was like dry ice inside his hands, the calcium deposits on his joints making him guarantees of pain to come. He soaked in the Epsom salt water for a long time, a washcloth over his eyes to drown out reality for a while. By the time he got out of the tub it was time to pick up Paige at the bus stop.

She was in a better mood today. She was quiet and somber, but that was better than the rage she'd been in the day before. She was her old self at least, no matter how disheartening that self could often be. Once back at the house, they had jerky and clementines, and then she went up to her room for a while. Tom stayed downstairs on the computer, a device that was almost entirely alien to him, wishing Betty were there to guide him through the perplexing world of the web, amongst other things.

When he'd had enough of searching for cattle auctions and watching equipment videos, he turned off the computer and went upstairs with his late wife still on his mind. He stepped into the bedroom—*their* bedroom—and sat on her old hope chest. It had the rich smell of venerable wood. Tom ran his fingertips across the golden studs that lined the edges, caressing this small part of her. Like the closet, the chest was still filled with her clothes and the blankets she'd knitted. He'd been unable to bear getting rid of his wife's things, aside from those that Dawn had taken, which mostly amounted to jewelry, much of which he'd bought for Betty for anniversaries. He knew he wasn't helping his grief move any faster by clinging to these things, but he wasn't going to sell the house either, and while it had once been a loving home it was now just a faded reflection of one, a tomb made of chipped paint and streaked windowpanes, a building where sad memories died slow.

On top of the dresser beside him was a row of framed photos, mostly of the kids—Dawn as little girl watering the lawn; Scott in his little league uniform; both of the kids on Halloween, Scott as the cartoon villain Skeletor and Dawn as a Disney princess Tom couldn't name. There was a photo of Dawn as an adult with her husband Leon. She was cradling baby Paige in her arms and the whole family was dressed in white and photographed in the soft light reserved for newborn photos. But the picture that always caught Tom's eye was of he and Betty at the beach in Corpus Christi, on their honeymoon in 1975. Betty had a motorized, folding Polaroid camera—all the rage at the time—and they'd asked a young woman to snap the shot. They were standing with a beautiful tangerine of a sunset swirling behind them like a surrealist oil painting. Betty was so young, so beautiful and healthy.

Why couldn't I have died first?

It was not the first time he'd had the thought.

Another thought that stalked him was the guilt he felt over missing Betty more than he missed Dawn. He did miss his daughter and lamented her death, and it was more painful to lose a daughter than a spouse. But Dawn had been her own woman for a long time. She'd been grown—out of the house and in charge of her own life, blessed with her own family. Her death was far more tragic, and yet it didn't leave the hole in his heart that Betty's passing did. Betty was the biggest part of his every day. She'd been with him for more than two thirds of his life. Her sudden absence was like a steel-toed kick to the heart, and the permanence of that absence was as black as a curse. Feeling more despair over his late wife than his late daughter, Tom grew disappointed in himself as a father. Perhaps his son was right to shun him. Maybe he hadn't been as close to his children as he should have been when they were young. Maybe he hadn't hugged and kissed them enough, too busy with ranch work and subduing his stress with a bottle.

From the top of the dresser the eyes of his family beamed, stars shining bright though they'd long ago died out, leaving just the echo of a gleaming farewell.

A rustle in the walk-in closet turned his head.

"Paige? That you in there?"

The closet's light was on, the door slightly ajar. He could make out the girl's small shadow inside, but she wasn't answering him, so he got up and opened the door.

"Whatcha doin in there?"

Paige stood in one of Betty's old evening gowns, the dazzling blue one Tom had always loved her in. It hung around Paige like a cloak, the scooped neck riding low on her belly, the sleeves swallowing her arms and hanging down like glittery tentacles. Around the girl's neck was a string of her grandmother's pearls. There was shame on her face. She seemed to think she was in trouble.

"Playin dress up?" he asked, smiling.

She hung her head.

"It's okay," he said. "I mean, you should ask before you go in my room, that's for sure. But you can play dress up with Nana's clothes if you wanna."

Paige's brow furled. "They're not her clothes. Not anymore. She's dead."

Her bluntness took him back a step.

Kids can be so cruel without meaning to be.

"They're still hers, Paige."

"Dead people can't have things. That's why they say *you can't take it with you.*"

"That may be true, but…"

"I like this dress."

"So did your Nana. It looks good on you. A little long maybe."

"I'll grow into it."

This made him chuckle. "How long you been doin this?"

"What?"

"Dressin up in here, silly."

"I dunno. I only do it sometimes."

"You like lookin all grown up, huh?"

She nodded, admiring herself in the mirror on the back of the door.

"I'll bet you and Alice liked to play dress up together." Tom wondered how safe it was to bring up the girl's name. He'd been thinking it would be better get Paige remembering the good times she'd had with her best friend, so that they wouldn't vanish under the heaviness of the tragedy. "Did y'all do that at her house?"

The girl's voice was soft and low. "It's part of our world."

"Oh yeah?"

"In Sopheria, we are beautiful."

"Sopheria? What's Sopheria?"

She looked down, rolling her fingers. "It's our world—our special world. I probably shouldn't tell you about it."

"How come?"

She shrugged.

"Secret, huh? Was that Alice's rule or yours?"

"It's just the rule of Sopheria. I only told you because I didn't want you to be mad about me using the dress. I need it for the ball."

He squinted. "Ball?"

"The Great Ball of Galilee. Princess Katandra is having a ball to celebrate her engagement to Sir Rowan. He is the bravest knight in all the land. He just came back from battle for a little while, but he has to go back after the ball."

"So there's a war on, huh?"

Tom admired her creativity and wanted to encourage it, but something about her continuing to play in a fantasyland she and Alice had created together made him tense and depressed all at once.

"The Dark Ones have gotten stronger," Paige said. "Rowan killed Og—he's the evil lion-wolf—but the Black Lord Slagon has tasted blood now, and soon all will be lost."

Tom's tension increased. The grim finality of her words sounded more appropriate for an adult novelist than a little girl.

"Well, all doesn't have to be lost, darlin," he said. "Rowan could save the day, right?"

"No. Not this time."

"Sure he could. It's your story, you could give it a happy ending."

"It's not up to me what happens."

"Well then, who's it up to? Wait, is this from a book you're readin?"

"No!" she said, face reddening. "Sopheria is the other world. It's the world *behind* the world. It's not just some story!"

Tom bit his lip. "Darlin, now you gotta know that this is all make-believe, right?"

Paige's face flushed and contorted. "Shut up! *You don't know anything!*"

She stormed out of the bedroom, nearly tripping herself on the dress.

"Stop right there, young lady!"

He wasn't about to let her sass him like that. He'd been letting a lot of things slide, but Paige had to be scolded for telling him to shut up. She reached her bedroom before he could get to her and slammed the door in his face. When he tried the doorknob it was already locked.

"Open this door," he said, getting no response.

For fifteen minutes he talked to her through the door, but she didn't reply. The lock on the other side was a simple one that took a flat, indistinct key. It could be popped open with a mere screwdriver. He thought about going to his toolbox, but decided against it. She was bound to get hungry by dinnertime and would have to come out at some point. When she did, she'd have to answer for her rotten behavior. He could wait.

And wait he did, long past dinner, long past bedtime.

Before he turned in he made one last try at it.

"Your dinner got cold," he said to the door. "If you're ready to apologize I'll heat it up for ya."

"I'm not hungry," Paige said, soft and distant.

"You got anythin else to say to your grandpa?"

There was a long pause.

"Sorry," she muttered.

It sounded halfhearted, but he was tired of the whole mess by now. He went to his bedroom and got out of his clothes rather slowly. He tossed in bed, thinking of lost income, mounting bills and Dr. White, the psychiatrist Paige needed to see more often.

CHAPTER EIGHTEEN

On Thursday Tom met with a financial planner and managed to get a few things in order. He didn't want to take out another damned loan. Mortgaging one's future is how his father went belly up, and he swore he'd never make the same mistakes as his old man. The new cattle would have a quick turnaround and should be able to get him through till spring. He dropped off steaks to individual buyers and managed to get back to the ranch before noon, giving him plenty of time to work before sundown.

Tom was home just long enough to eat lunch when the doorbell rang, and he was surprised to see his neighbor Fred Hollister standing on his porch. Tom welcomed the heavyset pecan farmer inside and Fred took off his cap, revealing thin, white hair that had become even sparser since they last talked.

"How you been, Fred?"

"Oh, all right. All right. How bout yourself?"

"The same, ya know. What brings ya around?"

"Well, Tom, I hope you don't think I'm buttin into your business here, but I thought you'd wanna know this."

"Whatcha got for me?"

The big man rolled his shoulders, his face long with concern. "Early this mornin, while you was out, a car pulled up in your driveway and a man got out and looked like he was snoopin round your house. I was eatin my breakfast and lookin out over the prairie like I do, and just happened to notice the car 'cause I'd never seen it round your place before, and your truck wasn't in the driveway, like I said. A'course I don't see so good these days, but I grabbed my binoculars I keep for my bird watchin."

"Well, hell, that is definitely somethin I wanna know about. You notice what kind of car? Was it a Lincoln?"

"Nah. It was some kinda utility vehicle, a bronco maybe. Silver. New-lookin."

It could still be Donati, Tom thought, *despite the different car.*

The idea that it might be Reston, or whoever had killed Alice, also entered his mind. It was a thought that curdled the blood in his veins.

"What about the guy? What'd he look like?"

"Big fella. Looked like a wrestler. Could tell he was muscular even in his coat. Had a back like a tractor."

"You said he was *snoopin* around?"

"I'd say he was. I saw him walkin round the house and then he headed for the barn."

"The barn?" Tom asked, his jaw tightening. "You see him go in? He mess with my livestock or horses?"

"No, no. He just sorta walked around it. I thought it looked fishy so I came out, but by the time I got dressed and made it over here he was up an' gone. I thought about puttin a call in to Dale over at the station but thought I'd get with you bout it first in case it was some friend a yours, or maybe a business partner or somethin like that."

Tom shook his head. "I don't think so."

"Me neither. But like I said, I wanted to be sure."

"I appreciate this, Fred. You're a good neighbor. You see this sumbitch again, just call the cops on him, okay?"

"Ayuh."

After checking on the barn and all the animals inside, making sure this visitor hadn't done any harm, Tom took to his chores, hoping they would clear his mind of the stress that had fallen upon him like a cancer. His nerves were wracked and it put a dull ache behind his eyes. As he toiled, his hair blew in the wind and he reminded himself to go to the barbershop and look civilized again. He dug holes and shuffled feed, thinking about the heat Sands had been applying and wondering if the new visitor was somehow linked to it.

Better that than him being linked to Alice's murder.

It enraged Tom that word had gotten out that Paige was at the scene of the crime. It put her at risk as a witness.

Maybe I should ask Dale for police protection, he thought. But somehow he didn't think it would be good for Paige psychologically. It would create an environment of fear around their home. In all likelihood, the visitor worked with Donati. Most investigators had some help these days, according to all those true crime shows on TV. The days of the lone private dick went out with the icebox and the cathedral radio. There were no more Sam Spades or Milton Arbogasts, not even in the movies.

Whoever the guy was, he had circled the barn more than once. His footprints gave him away. And more than that he had circled the house and the mini-barn where the fresh cattle were quarantined. But what concerned Tom the most was the set of prints that led away from the ranch and wound down the slope and into the dark, spindly tunnel of the woods.

⤳

Dale wasn't in, so Tom left a message with the receptionist, but he didn't give any details. Beyond the trespassing at his barn, Tom thought the sheriff would want to know about anybody messing around in those woods.

When he picked Paige up from the bus stop it was already growing colder, as if night was going to come extra early, dragging with it the bruising weight of winter air. When she ran to the truck he thought she was just trying to escape the chill, but he then saw the misery on her face and knew she'd had another rough day.

"Them brats botherin you again?"

She pushed air out of her nostrils in a huff. "I just wanna go home."

They drove in silence for a while, Tom's anger toward her bullies marinating.

"I think maybe we really should go to the boxin gym," he said. "These lil bastards need to learn a lesson. I can even set up a heavy bag in the utility shed. Get you some gloves. My old sixteen-ouncers are probably too big for ya but—"

"*I just want to go home!*"

He bit his lip against her tone and they drove on, silence draped over them like wet rugs. When they pulled into the driveway, she jumped out of the truck before it was all the way stopped and ran to the door, opening it with the key he'd given her for emergencies. He cursed to himself and slammed the door on his way down from the truck, and then did the same to the one on the house.

He'd had enough.

"We need to talk about this, young lady!"

Paige was upstairs, walking quickly down the hall to her room, and as Tom followed her he realized she was crying. It made him stop in his tracks because it was so unlike her. She was always so stoic—cold, even. This sudden showing of emotion gave him pause, but he managed to reach the door before she could lock it. He wasn't about to go through that again. When he got into the room, Paige was in the bed, face first into her pillows, a groundhog burrowing to safety from the wolves out to pick her bones clean. She was lying on her tiger and its head popped out from under her chest, a goony smile on its stitched face. Tom sat on the edge and his granddaughter rolled over to face away from him, her little shoulders quaking beneath her pink hoodie. He put his hand on her back and was relieved she didn't try to shake him off.

"I think we need to go see Dr. White again," he said.

Her sobbing had slowed and her voice was near a whisper, her nostrils still wet.

"That's not until next week," she said.

"I think we should go more often, honey. There's a lotta stuff we need to work through."

She was silent, and then she shocked him again, harder this time. Paige's voice was low. "I'm not crazy."

Tom had no reply. The weight of what she had said held the intensity of galaxies in just three soft-spoken words. There was such adult hurt in them, such self-doubt and heartsickness. Once again the maturity of his granddaughter's problems reached into him and twisted all that was inside, and a great wealth of sadness spread through the wound it had torn, giving him more than his share of sorrow to live off of.

"Nobody thinks that," he told her.

Paige turned to look at him. Her eyes were bloodshot, irises two bottomless mineshafts, brown darkness that swallowed all the light of the world.

"You're wrong, Grandpa. Everyone thinks that. Even you."

The ringing phone interrupted them.

He held her gaze until she put her head back down on the pillow. "I'll be right back," he said.

Tom didn't want to leave her side just then, but if it was a supplier or customer he simply couldn't afford to miss the call.

"Hello?" he asked into the receiver.

"Mr. Hargrave?"

It was a man's voice he didn't recognize.

"Ayuh. Who's this?"

"My name is Paul Godfrey. My boys go to school with your granddaughter."

"Yes, of course. We share the same bus stop."

"That's right, sir. That's why I'm calling, actually."

"Oh?"

"My sons just got home and Mark, my oldest, told me something that concerns Paige that I thought you should know."

Tom braced himself. "Oh?"

"Yeah. He told me that while they were waiting for the bus to pull into the loop at the front of the school this afternoon, a man came up to Paige and started talking to her. Mark said he wasn't a teacher or anybody they recognized. He said he was a stranger."

Something cold slithered up Tom's spine. "A stranger? What was he talkin to her about?"

"Mark said he was asking her about Alice MacDougall."

"Jesus."

"I thought you should know. Mark says this guy just drove up like all the parents do and got out of the car and started in on her. Says the guy came at her pretty hard too, made her pretty upset."

"Son of a bi—oh, um, sorry."

"Hell, I'd be swearing too."

"Did Mark tell you anythin else? Like what he looked like?"

"Said it was an older guy wearing a suit. At first he thought he was a cop, but then when he started berating her…"

Donati. Goddamned Donati.

"What exactly did he say to her?"

"I don't know his exact words. Mark just said he was asking about Alice, their friendship and what Paige had… you know… *seen*."

Tom clenched the phone. "Where the hell was the faculty? Why didn't anyone intervene?"

"Apparently the crossing guard noticed when the guy got loud, but when she tried to get over to him through the traffic the guy saw her and hopped in his car and pulled off."

"What car?"

"Well, the car he came in."

"No, I mean what kind of car. Was it a Lincoln?"

"No, sir. Mark says it was an SUV. And he said somebody else was driving it. Some real big guy."

The big wrestler. I knew it. They're in this together, the sons of bitches.

"Anything else, Mr. Godfrey?"

"Sorry, that's it. But it sure concerns my wife and me. I plan on having a talk with the principal."

"Ayuh, me too."

"Sounds good. I'll be calling him in the morning."

Tom thanked him. They hung up and Tom leaned against the wall, his head hung low. Despite a small sense of appreciation that he still had some allies left in this town, his heart ached for Paige and seethed anger toward Sands. He resisted the urge to punch a hole right through the damned drywall. Sensing his mood, Jep came over, tail limp, and gave him a sympathy whine. Tom patted him as the dog nuzzled into his leg.

I've got to get a hold of Dale. This is stalking now, plain and simple.

He collected himself and on his way through the living room he paused near the liquor cabinet, forgetting it had been emptied long ago. Had so much as a drop of whiskey been hiding in there, he might have had a relapse right then. He was grateful Betty had filled it with old scrapbooks. Though she'd never said it, he knew she'd chosen them for the cabinet because they were filled with pictures of the ones he loved, ones he didn't want to let down again. She was good at subtleties like that, the kind of woman that gently tried to cure her husband's faults without harshly shaming him by pointing them out.

As he moved through the dim hallway, he ran one hand over his face, his fingertips stopping on his lips as if they were sealing in a battle cry. Tom had a limit, and he'd not so much been pushed past it as he was launched beyond it by an atomic blast.

When he reached Paige's door it was closed. He knocked before opening it a crack. She was still on the bed, but now she had a notebook out and was writing. The notebook was covered in a fuzzy, purple coating and bejeweled with plastic diamonds and rubies. When she saw him she scurried to push it under her pillow and he pretended not to have noticed.

"Paige, I want you to tell me about the man who talked to you today."

Her face pinched like an anteater.

"Was it the man who was in our driveway just the other day?"

She nodded.

"Why didn't you tell me he came up to you at the school?"

"I dunno."

He wanted to shake her, frustrated by her apathy. Instead he stood there, speaking calmly, mimicking what he'd seen Dr. White and the interviewer Emma Rowe do to successfully get the truth out of Paige.

"Listen to me. If he or *anybody* else comes to you askin about Alice, you need to tell me right away. And if any stranger approaches you when I'm not around, you *scream* for help from an adult."

"Okay."

Tom ran his hand over the back of his neck. He wished he knew what else to do. Grilling her about it would just upset her more, and while he wanted to know the exact questions Donati had asked, he already had a good idea what they were. Best to wait and have her tell it all to Dale anyway. But another part of him wanted answers while the incident was still fresh in her mind. It infuriated him to feel this way, to feel like no matter what step he took it would be the wrong one and in the wrong direction, that breaking these impasses would only plunge him deeper into this abyss, dragging his poor granddaughter with him.

"I'm gonna fix this so nobody bothers you again," he said. "Don't you worry, darlin. I won't let nobody scare you no more, and nobody's gonna hurt you, I promise."

He left on that note, closing the door behind him as he stepped back into the shadowy sorrow of the hallway, toward his room where he could whisper to Betty in private.

That night, the barn burned.

CHAPTER NINETEEN

He awoke to screaming.

Tom's first thought was that it must be Paige. His adrenaline skyrocketed, launching him out of bed in sheer panic, but as more screams filled the night, Tom realized they weren't human. They were the wet, garbled throat-shrieks of cattle, mewling in pain, terror or both. The window to his left had an orange glow like a sunset, and he dashed to it for only a second before spinning around, the sight outside causing him to charge downstairs. He rushed into his boots so fast that he stumbled, nearly breaking his ankle before catching himself and putting a hole in the drywall. He didn't change out of his pajamas; he just threw on his overcoat, took an extinguisher from the hall and ran out the door, running toward the frenzied inferno of the barn.

Black smoke rose into the night sky in billowy blankets, the whole ranch illuminated by the towering blaze. The main barn was a fury of fire. The flames lapped through the slats and had climbed all the way up, setting the edge of the roof ablaze. One side of the barn was concaved, the same wood-rotted spot he'd been patching up. In the pasture, a few cows were running, having somehow escaped, possibly through the hole. One of them was trotting in frantic circles, screeching, its body engulfed in flames. From inside the barn came the panicking cries of the livestock and horses, and at the wall where Essie's stable was the planks shuddered as the horse kicked at it in an effort to escape.

The flaming bossie was charging too violently for Tom to get close enough to spray it with the extinguisher, and he had to prioritize. Getting to the barn before the roof was fully swallowed by fire was his objective, so he ran at full force, his knees grinding and popping as they were put to use in a way they hadn't in many years. The snow grabbed at his boots, trying to suck him into the earth, and he stumbled more than once before reaching the barn. He was cautious of a back draft so he butted the door with the end of the extinguisher and stepped aside, spraying the flames that greeted with the roar of a lion.

The inside of the barn was like a vision of hell. The smoke was stifling, crushing his lungs, nearly thick enough to blind him. A few more of the cows were on fire, still trapped in their pens, kicking and screaming as they were burned alive. Tom went to Essie's gate first, ducking behind it as he let her out so not to be kicked to death. The horse bolted away in a full gallop. Tom went to the gates of the other cattle that were still unharmed, putting them first, and kept the gate between he and them as one by one they charged out of the barn and into the field in one long, mooing convoy. He sprayed the burning cattle with the extinguisher, gagging on the black mist as he doused them and then let them free. Some were able to flee while others were already unconscious or dead, their bodies charred and still smoldering. The stench of their charred flesh hung in the air like bog gas.

At the end of the row was Hondo's stable, an infuriated, bright box of flame that gave no hope that the pony was still alive.

There were a few other engulfed cows that were still screeching behind their gates when Tom had to run from the barn for his own safety, having no choice but to leave them to burn. The ceiling was awash in fire, the flames devouring the barn in ravenous, red tongues. Every bracing pole had flames coiling around them like flickering tentacles. He didn't want to leave a single cow behind, but he also didn't want to be inside when the roof collapsed.

Running out into the field, Tom noticed headlights in his driveway. He ran toward the vehicle, rage propelling him through the slush, but he soon realized the driver was not backing out, but pulling in. He also noticed that either one of the cows or Essie—or possibly a human culprit—had burst through the horse fence and barbwire, creating a pathway into the road for all of the terrified cattle that wanted to get as far away from the inferno as possible. Most of them were already in the street, some wandering mindlessly while others were running down the road, still in terror. Essie was nowhere in sight. Tom pursued them, going toward the truck that had pulled up to the fence. Two men were backlit against the floodlights mounted on the truck. Tom wished he had his shotgun.

"Jesus, Tom!" one of them said.

He recognized the voice of Fred Hollister. Tom moaned with relief.

"Call 911!" he shouted.

"Already did," said the other man as he stepped forward. As he got closer Tom could see that it was Fred's son, Willard. "They're on the way."

"We could hear the ruckus all the way over at the farm," Fred said.

"Saw the blaze and came right over."

Tom nodded. "You're a good friend, Fred."

Having been a rancher himself before turning to nut farming, Fred didn't need instruction and took his own initiative. He'd pulled a rope from his truck and was already making a lariat.

"They're spooked bad," Tom said. "We need to pass em up and block off the road."

"I'm on it," said Willard, climbing into the Dodge Ram.

Fred removed a box of tools and some more rope, then got out of the cab, letting Willard gun it, the truck ripping along the shoulder, going around the herd so he could turn the truck around to face them with the floodlights on, which would stop them and make it easier for Tom and Fred to see.

"I'm gonna get my prod," Tom said. "Just try an wrangle em for a minute."

He ran up to the utility shed and flung the door open, cursing himself for not remembering where he'd left the cattle prod. He just hadn't used it recently. Hopefully it still had some juice. Finding it near the sledgehammer, Tom grabbed it and a flashlight and headed up to the house. He whistled and Jep came running out, amped up by all the excitement. Paige's voice came from the upstairs hall and Tom told her firmly to stay in the house. He ran down the driveway and spilled back into the street where Fred and Willard were doing their best to wrangle the crazed herd and guide them back into the grazing field. If they could just get a few of them going, the rest would follow.

Tom moved into the undulating livestock and began prodding the beasts while Jep, a trained herding dog, entered the throng and immediately began nipping at the heels of the cattle, sending them in the same direction. Fred had lassoed two wild ones and they were complying as he flicked his wrists, having long ago learned the rule of the rope. At the rear, Willard was circling the sluggish ones, nudging them into the crowd with his arms stretched as wide as they'd go. The chaos made a headcount nearly impossible, as did the untold number of fatalities in the barn, but Tom felt that they'd managed to gather them all together and none had strayed too far from home. Essie, however, might still be running, still in a panic. Tom knew very well how easily horses could be overtaken by fear, how all of their training could fly out their brains when they thought they were in danger. He had to find his horse, but first they had to finish with the herd and fix the fence.

In the distance, the sweet sound of a fire truck wailed like a demon, flooding Tom with relief. The snow had kept the fire from spreading to the quarantine barn, but if it managed to reach the propane tanks his troubles would multiply at an alarming rate. Within the black fog, ash fell like snow flurries, and against the backdrop of the night sky orange embers twirled in the breeze.

"Round em!" Tom called to Jep.

The dog began barking, leaping on his hind legs as he snapped at the cattle more fiercely, ushering them into the frosted corral. Willard climbed back into to the truck and drove up to the fence as the last of the livestock were wrangled back inside, using the big Dodge to block off the hole by parking it right on the edge.

Tears welled in Tom's eyes, casting reflections of fire on his cheeks. His heart was thudding away like a woodpecker, limbs quaking, his mouth a desert as he watched the barn bow, break and crash into the ground with thunder and sparks, making the cattle go wild again. They were confined now, and once the initial surprise of the barn collapsing passed they settled down, far enough away from the fire to feel comfortable, though still weary and spooked. A plume of smoke rolled across the field and scurried into the surrounding woods like a legion of rats. Ash filled the sky, twinkling.

Tom turned to his neighbors. "Y'all really saved my ass."

On top of the ridge, he could see red lights spinning, a twirling carnival of rescue. The fire truck was not alone. Police cars and an ambulance escorted it in a flickering formation that perforated the night.

Fred stepped beside Tom and put a hand on his shoulder. He was so close that Tom could smell his morning breath, backed by a hint of last night's whiskey.

"This wasn't no accident, was it, Tom?"

Tom didn't meet his neighbor's gaze. He just looked across his ranch, silent, counting his remaining cattle, watching his incinerated barn implode. When he finally had to look away, he glanced at Fred, but a small light over the man's shoulder caught Tom's eye.

He saw the front door of the house was open a crack, the yellow light of the foyer shining out. Silhouetted in that sliver was Paige, a motionless shadow, a cardboard cutout of a little girl.

PART THREE

FAMILY VALUES

CHAPTER TWENTY

A young police officer drove Tom up and down the road in search of Essie. The horse's saddle had burned in the fire but Tom had an old spare that he kept in the utility shed. He held it in his lap now, along with his lariat, staring out into the snowy meadow, looking for a shape, a shadow or hoof prints. A thin sliver of pink light was bleeding on the horizon, puncturing the low clouds in its promise of daylight.

A shuffling mass appeared in a low spot of the passing basin. Tom told the officer to stop the car. He ran out with his saddle slung over his shoulder by the pommel, holding the lariat with both hands, the spoke in his right and the coil in his left, still clutching a handful of sugar cubes.

Essie was moving slowly through the bowed valley. She looked majestic against the fallen snow, like a scene from a dream or movie. Tom knew she would still be shaken by what had happened, so he moved cautiously, cooing to her with gentle words, his voice revealing none of the anxiety that hammered in his chest.

In the dip of the valley's bowl the snow was thicker, hard enough to have slight resistance before plunging his feet into deep, icy pits that chilled him through his boots. As he got closer he made clicking noises with his tongue, letting Essie know that he had treats for her. The horse turned an ear at him and he made sure to stay on one side of her instead of approaching her head on.

Inching forward, he saw the horse's mane, blackened by fire and smoke, and the burns that shined wetly on one side of her. It looked as if a flaming board must have fallen on her from the rafters of the barn. Tom winced seeing them, knowing she must be in great pain. If he caught her, there was no way he could ride her back to the ranch as he had planned.

Through the loop of his lariat he put one hand forward, holding the cubes. Essie resisted at first, still unnerved by what had happened, but the more he cooed and clicked the calmer she became, her snorts fewer and farther between. Tom didn't rush her, and kept the police officer waiting for almost twenty minutes as he stood beside Essie, slowly stroking her. When she finally showed interest in the cubes he put his hand through the loop in the lariat again, placing the rope around her neck with his other hand as she moved her head into the loop to get her treat. She didn't buck or struggle. She knew Tom was with her now and things were going to be all right.

"You mind takin this saddle back to the house?" he asked the officer once he'd come back to the road, leading Essie by the rope.

"You ain't gonna ride her?"

"She's burned and spooked senseless."

"Oh. Sorry."

"I think she'll be okay, but I'm gonna walk her home."

The policeman blinked. "It must be over a mile, and it's ten degrees out here."

"I know it."

He'd dressed before they left and figured he could tolerate the cold for a while. He didn't really have a choice. He had a horse trailer that could be towed by a 4X4, but it was very old and the bottom had rusted out last spring, and he'd had no real need to get another one. Some of his distant neighbors may have one, but he didn't want to bother them at this hour.

"You sure?" the officer asked.

"I'm sure. I figure I can do it in under forty-five minutes. I won't freeze to death."

—✕—

Tom spoke with the officials, as did Fred and Willard. The fire was extinguished well before any further damage could be done, but police and firefighters remained on his property as dawn bloomed over the tops of the trees. A blossom of pink rose within the withered limbs, a splotch of cotton candy riddled with spiders.

He spoke with the fire investigator the longest. The woman treated the barn like a crime scene, trying to determine the source of the fire. Before the sun could appear, Dale Rogers showed up and Tom made coffee, having anticipated his arrival.

They went through everything: the fire, Donati and his visit, as well as his appearance at the school, and of course the big, unknown man and how he had snooped around the barn. Tom told Dale about the stranglehold Sands had been putting on him and how he'd been intimidating people around town into turning a cold shoulder to Tom. His voice filled with the gravel of frustration, his anger turning his words to acid in his mouth, making him spit them out like venom.

"Whether this fire was arson or not, you need to tell those people to back off. They've got this private dick stalkin my granddaughter, questionin her without my permission or even havin me present. They've got some big lug trespassin on my property. I don't care how much cash this Sands fella has to throw around. Bein rich don't give him immunity, does it?"

Dale's face was ashen. "No. It doesn't. This will all be addressed. And there will be an investigation."

"Christ, Dale, why the hell these people wanna pressure us like this? What the hell is wrong with em?"

Dale leaned back in his chair and folded his hands. "They think Paige knows more than she's lettin on. They might even think she… well…" The sheriff hesitated, his eyes downcast.

Tom leaned forward. "What?"

"They might even think that she might've had somethin to do with it."

Tom's fists balled, teeth going tight as he had no words to express his anger.

"They also seem to think that maybe I'm not doin all I can to bring Alice's killer to justice," Dale said, "because I've known you for so long."

Tom tapped the table with his finger. "You know somethin? I'm startin to think these people protest too much. Ain't it true that in most child murder cases, usually someone in the kid's own family is at fault?" He didn't like himself for saying these things, but his outrage had warped his judgment, making him vent with all he had. "Maybe that's why they're so desperate to pin it on somebody else."

"In child murder cases, yes, the family is thoroughly looked into, and that's just what we're doin. The whole family's been interviewed at length, and our investigation is ongoin. But what I really wanna look into now is this Donati character and his little helper."

"You and me both."

"Let me handle it, Tom."

Tom was surprised Dale would say that, but given the speed and volume of his rant, he guessed he couldn't blame the sheriff.

"You know I will," he said. "You know I will."

Tom had left the front door open a crack, but the fire investigator knocked on it once before stepping into the house. She came to the table where they sat, her clipboard clutched against her yellow coat with the giant letters on it—FIRE INSPECTOR. A small walkie-talkie buzzed at her collar.

"We may be looking at spontaneous combustion," she said.

Tom's jaw fell. "Are you kiddin me? Ain't that science fiction?"

"No, sir. It does happen. Like all ranches there is a lot of organic waste here, and natural gas. That can lead to spontaneous combustion."

Dale nodded in agreement.

"So is that what you think happened?" Tom asked.

"Possibly," she said.

"You don't think it could've been arson?"

"That's also possible, but the problem is by extinguishing a fire the evidence of arson can be destroyed. I can't find any evidence of an incendiary fire, but that doesn't mean it didn't happen. The barn has also collapsed, and unfortunately that only adds to the spoliation."

Tom put his elbows on the table, dropping his head into his hands.

"We're still sifting through the rubble," she said. "But as of right now, it's all very vague."

⤬

The department was too small for Dale to offer twenty-hour police surveillance of the ranch, but he did promise that patrol cars would do regular drive-bys. By midmorning the fire engines and police cars had cleared out, as had Fred and Willard. Tom nailed a slab of plywood in front of the hole in the fence until he could repair it later in the day. With everyone gone, he was left alone with the wreckage and his newfound fears.

But he wasn't totally alone.

During the chaos, Paige had stayed in her room as asked. Now she was downstairs for breakfast. It was only Cheerios. Tom couldn't muster the energy to cook so much as an egg today. He wasn't just tired from a lack of sleep, he was tired from the whole series of events that had lead him to this broken state. There had been so much loss, so much ruination.

He called the vet's office and left a message about Essie. He hoped he could get a house call as soon as possible. For the time being he put aloe on her wounds and gave her some pain medicine. He would have to find a solution to the loss of the barn as quickly as possible, for he had no other place to stable her or keep the herd, and in this winter weather that spelled uncompromising doom. Maybe he could rent space from another ranch until he could get a new barn up and replace all the equipment that had been destroyed. All of this would be more money that he didn't have. He had no idea how long it would take for the insurance company to pay up, and in this situation he didn't have time to wait for bureaucrats to drag their lazy asses.

He gave Jep an extra-large breakfast for all of his hard work and told Paige he needed to lie down for a while. She reminded him that it was Friday; she had school. In all of the confusion he'd somehow thought it was Saturday. He told her to finish eating and then get dressed. They'd missed the bus, so he would have to drive her. That was alright by him, though. It would give him a chance to complain to the principal about how Paige had been berated by a stranger on school property.

The truck had cocooned the brutal cold during the night and getting in was like entering an igloo. He turned on the heat, feeling the arctic touch of the steering wheel even through his wool gloves. Beside him, Paige stared at the rubble of the barn as they backed out, and continued staring at it as they drove, turning her head until it was out of sight.

"What happened?" she asked.

"Just a fire."

"But how did it happen?"

"I don't know, honey. I just don't know."

She asked about the horses and the livestock and he told her about the dead cattle, and about Hondo. He saw a darkness cross over her face and then settle behind her eyes when she learned of the pony's death. He assured her that Essie would be all right and that the ranch had retained the majority of the herd. Things would be okay. He wanted her to believe it just as much as he wanted to believe it himself. Maybe if he said it aloud to enough people, it could somehow make it true.

The pink light of dawn had vanished under the clouds, leaving the sky an all-too-familiar slate color. It was misting and the windshield wipers droned as they fluttered across the glass. Warm air finally began to seep from the vents, allowing Tom's mind to think of something other than how damned cold he was. He still hadn't really warmed up from his long walk back to the ranch with Essie. The cold had settled into his bones, enveloping them with its cruelty. There had been no breeze, and he had been mighty grateful for that, but the air was bitter and there was little comfort in his layers of clothing. He soaked his feet in the tub when he got back, which had helped some, but the dull ache lingered in his body, clinging to him like an ex-lover that can't accept that it's over.

He knew he had to ask. It would eat at him if he didn't.

"Paige?"

"Yeah?"

"Is there anythin you might've forgotten to tell the police about what happened in them woods, anythin at all? I mean, is there somethin you're too scared to tell em?"

She turned her head away and stared out her window, silent, somber.

"I thought that maybe if there was, you might be more comfortable just tellin me instead of the police."

More silence.

"Maybe there was somethin more that happened? Maybe there was another person there? Did Alice say anythin weird the days before it happened? Was she scared about anythin?"

He looked at her so long that he drifted off into the shoulder, the bumper scraping into the snow mounds before he righted the truck. Luckily they were alone on the road.

"Alice was scared," she said, making him hold his breath. "She was afraid of what Slagon might do."

"Who?"

"The Black Lord Slagon."

"Damnit, Paige! I ain't talkin about your stupid fairy stories!" He hit the brakes. "This is serious, young lady! Alice is dead, damnit! *Dead!* And you're talkin to me about make-believe monsters? You're old enough to know better. You're old enough to know the goddamned difference between what's real and what ain't."

She turned away from him again and this time he didn't mind the silence. It was better than listening to her childish nonsense. He'd let Dr. White decipher that. He'd had more than enough aggravation for one day, and it wasn't even noon yet.

CHAPTER TWENTY-ONE

When he tried to see the school principal, Tom was told he would need to make an appointment. He grew frustrated listening to the lack of availability and told the assistant he'd just call later to schedule it. But it was for the best. He was already boiling over from everything that had happened today and would only end up taking it out on the poor principal.

Back home, Fred Hollister came to Tom's rescue once again. He had two old boxcars on his land, combined and customized to hold and dispense feed for his ranch horses. The boxcars were rusted and in need of repair, but they would keep Essie and the livestock warm and sheltered until Tom could have a new barn constructed. He would have to do short cattle drives from Fred's land to his and back each day, but it was a temporary solution Tom was extremely grateful for. He suggested he pay monthly rent but Fred would not have it. Tom told the farmer he'd brought their relationship to a new level and that he was proud to call a man as good as him a friend. He decided that when he came back later in the day to tend to the cattle he would be bringing Fred a big bag full of steaks from the freezer.

Having transferred the herd to the boxcar barn, Tom secured them in their pens and stepped down, sealing the door behind him. The day was clear and the sun was at work on the snow, revealing the silted earth that sulked in gray misery beneath. He peered toward the copse of trees that lined the valley like a rotted fence. He felt terribly enervated, spent. Trenching up the bluff, Tom's mind tortured him with the gory image of the little girl he'd found within those woods. The police had been in and out of them a dozen times. By now there was no more evidence to obtain.

Could there be more to this than Paige has let on?

Maybe there really was something she'd left out, either because of fear or confusion, or possibly she'd omitted something without even realizing it. The moment Tom had seen the body was somewhat of a blur. His adrenaline had started pumping, shock rattling him like thunder, making for a hazy recollection at best. If he had thin memories of the moment, he could only image how distorted Paige's recollection of the events might be. She'd actually seen the girl get killed. Her shock was a deeper, blacker thing, her fear palpable and cold. It only made sense that something might have slipped through the netting of her mind.

But what little piece could that have been?

Clearly her memory of the killer was weak. She was able to give a rough description of him but was unable to positively identify him as Reston. Above all else, discovering and capturing the killer was most important. Tom wondered what further steps were being made in the investigation. There was only so much Dale could disclose to him.

Still, he couldn't help but wonder about the bizarre behavior of the MacDougall family and Sands. Why such hostility toward Paige? She'd been Alice's best friend. The MacDougalls knew her well. She was an odd duck, for sure, but she wasn't a bad seed. Christ, she was just a little girl. If she was withholding information, Tom was sure she wouldn't be doing it maliciously. But the family's persistence in the matter did make Tom curious.

And then there was all of Paige's fairy talk—all this nonsense about the "Black Lord". It seemed like she was bringing it up more and more.

Maybe she's just trying to change the subject when I talk about Alice. Maybe it's some kind of coping mechanism.

His mind flashed back to when he had come into her room and found her writing in the purple notebook. *Purple. Alice's favorite color.* It was one of many notebooks Paige had brought along with her whenever she and Alice played. He remembered how she had dashed to hide it from him.

Little girls and their secrets.

He headed for home, moving faster now.

~~

Most of the writing was just what he expected. Flowery and juvenile, yet sweet and creative, in the vein of *The Lord of the Rings* but with a touch of Disney princess tales. Some of it was in Paige's handwriting and some of it was in what he guessed was Alice's, up until the last few entries, which were all written by Paige. She had continued their saga. The tales told of love and war, but a lot of the wordage was confusing to Tom, for it seemed that the girls had created their own lexicon for this world called Sopheria, a new language for their characters to speak in. It was meshed with English and even had a touch of French, which was always in Alice's writing.

It seemed the girl had studied it.

When he came to the chapters about The Dark Ones, Tom found them incredibly grim, particularly for being written by young girls. There were amphibious monsters that hunted children, bloodthirsty demons looking to impregnate virgins. One beast with tentacles named Vodin was a rapist; not in so many words, but clearly a sexual predator. The illustrations the girls had made, though childish, were chillingly vivid.

And then there was The Black Lord Slagon.

He was the embodiment of evil, a being concocted by a black witch who combined drops of the blood of all of the villains of Sopheria. He was described as incredibly tall and lanky, black-clad with long hair and a featureless face—no ears or mouth, only two eyes that were entirely white, as pale as his chalky face. Like some of the other characters, the girls had drawn pictures of him, but unlike the others these pictures were done entirely in black crayon. They made Tom shiver. He wasn't sure why he found them so disturbing. Maybe it was the idea of two little girls coming up with something so horrific that did it.

But what concerned him most of all was that all of the writing pertaining to the Black Lord Slagon, the beasts Og and Vodin, and the rest of the malevolent Dark Ones, were all in Paige's handwriting. The two girls may have come up with these parts of the story together, but Paige wrote all the horror chapters. And more than this, all of the writing Paige had done after Alice died was entirely about the Dark Ones. The heroes and princess appeared to be getting killed off by Slagon and his minions in a slow genocide. Here the violence was graphic, gruesome and twisted, and what made it all the more bizarre was how Paige was completely destroying this world she and Alice had created, a world she spoke of so fondly.

Maybe she's destroying it because it can't go on without Alice.

In those last twenty or so pages, The Black Lord Slagon had conquered the Castle of Light where Princess Katandra lived. While Sir Rowan was away fighting battles against the encroaching horde of Dark Ones, Slagon took Katandra from her tower and carried her out into a snowy patch of woods. There he had set up an altar, and he laid her down upon it and sacrificed her to the demons.

The way he killed the princess was by stabbing her repeatedly in the stomach, with a broadsword.

CHAPTER TWENTY-TWO

He told himself it was nothing. The child was just recreating the horror she'd seen in order to process it. But the dark tone the story had taken without Alice as a co-author was very disconcerting. Was it a sign of depression, or possibly an unhealthy obsession with the macabre?

But it's just fiction, Tom. Hell, Stephen King is a household name. It's not all that weird for somebody to be writing horror stories.

But a ten-year-old girl?

That Paige could even dream up such awful things put a twitch in Tom's eyelids. That her mind was filled with such darkness, such violence...

He picked up the phone.

⌒

"I don't blame you for being upset," Mary said. "My God, this is all so awful: the murder, that private investigator, the barn burning down. I'm so sorry, Tom."

"At least all that makes some sorta sense, no matter how terrible it is. But this fairy story of hers... I think that's what's gettin to me more than anythin else."

"I won't lie. It's disturbing. I'd be concerned too."

Tom sighed. "I'm not sure if I should try and talk to her about it or not. I mean, I invaded her privacy. I'm not proud of it, but I felt like it was the right thing to do given the circumstances. But if she finds out I snooped in her private things, she'll be sore as hell at me. I don't wanna lose her trust, ya know?"

"Yes. I know."

"You ever read any of your kids' diaries or notes?"

"No. Not that I can recall."

As usual when he called Mary, he came back to the same old question.

"How do you think Betty would handle this?"

He heard Mary take a deep breath. "She wasn't as perfect as you remember her, Tom. In a situation like this, I think she'd be just as confused as you are."

CHAPTER TWENTY-THREE

After speaking with his insurance adjuster, as well as the bank, Tom headed out to Maynard, as much to take his mind off things as to buy some much needed supplies. He was getting his feed and tools there now that Ed Green had barred him, making him go outside of Middlebury for the ranch's necessities. It was the next town over, but luckily their farm and feed store were not that far across the border. He'd have plenty of time to drive there, shop, and get back in time to pick up Paige at the bus stop.

He pulled out of the driveway and headed to rural Route 12 out of Coyote Valley. The morning sunshine had died out again, suffocated by sluggish, rolling clouds that teased more snow. The air was crisp and distilled, and Tom loved the taste of it at the back of his throat. Cold days, cruel as they could be, were refreshing, and Tom had always enjoyed how a man could own the world around him on a winter day. Most people shut themselves indoors, leaving everything vacant, quiet and contemplative.

Used to having this desolate road to himself on weekdays, Tom was a little surprised to see a car pull off of a side street and onto the route behind him. He shrugged it off, lost in thought, on autopilot. He veered left at the fork and took the route north toward Maynard. The car behind him did the same. It was closer now. Tom was able to identify the make and model. His teeth closed on each other.

A black Lincoln Town Car.

He hit the brakes, tires screaming, and the rear of the truck came up, bucking like a mad horse. The car skidded sideways in an effort not to hit him, swiping the dusted asphalt, and Tom put his truck in park and got out. He strode toward the car with balled fists, seeing Donati behind the wheel, a look of worry in his eyes when he saw the fury in Tom's.

It was rare that Tom got this angry, or at least it was these days. He'd mellowed with age, the angst of his youth having faded into a mildly embarrassing afterthought, distant and rusty, gladly left behind. But whenever he felt angry enough for violence, his mind rewound, refreshing memories of being in the ring, slugging away in the final rounds against a worthy opponent. That was when the pain had always made him extra lethal, when every breath stabbed his ribs as he blinked away the blood the cut-man hadn't been able to keep out of his eyes. That was when boxing went from a sport of respect to a battle of warriors, when it really became a fight. As he approached the car, he could almost feel the glove leather stretching taught across his knuckles and smell the adrenaline chloride swabs being stuffed into his nostrils to open the blowholes.

He was surprised that Donati hadn't thought to lock the door. Tom pulled it open and grabbed the man by the collar. The detective wasn't wearing his seatbelt, and Tom was able to drag him from the car and sling him to the gravel, dropping him like a bag of sand. Donati gasped as the air left his lungs and as he struggled to get up Tom came at him. Donati put his hands up in front of him, not in an act of self-defense but in a submissive pose that seemed to say *please, take it easy*.

"You dirty son of a bitch," Tom growled.

"I'm just doing my job, mister."

"Harassin my kid at school? That's your goddamned job?"

"It was just a couple of questions."

"You've got no right! No right at all! I'm her guardian. You wanna talk to her, you talk to me first."

"Hey now," Donati said, rising to his feet. He brushed himself off. "You told me to get lost."

"Damn right! But ya didn't. No, not you. You just keep pressin. And now you've got some gorilla workin with you too. What's his name?"

Donati didn't offer it.

Tom sneered. "Yeah, I figured your lips would get tight, especially after what happened this mornin."

"Listen, I heard about that. I assure you my associate and I had *nothing* to do with your barn."

"Well, all I know is that big boy was sniffin around my property the other day, and now I'm short one barn, one pony, and a fistful of cattle. You think it's all right to let animals burn to death?"

"Of course not. I'm telling you, we had nothing to do with it. He just came to ask you a few questions. You weren't home, so he checked around the barn to see if you were in there. That's it and that's all. We were clear on the other side of town when your barn burned."

"And just how do you know that?"

Donati's brow furrowed. "Know what?"

"What time the barn burned?"

Donati fell silent, his hands outstretched in a small shrug, and Tom felt a mean heat rise in his chest, rush into his blood, and pour through every muscle and nerve fiber. To his astonishment, Donati smiled, about to say something, and Tom found himself turning sideways, rising on the balls of his feet, his right arm hooking toward the smug look on the other man's face.

Tom had always heard that the punch was the last thing to go on a fighter. Now he found out it was true.

He hit Donati so hard he nearly broke his hand. The man's head snapped back, his eyes closed before he even hit the ground. He crashed into the shoulder of the road, his skull smacking the gravel with a revolting crack, sounding like a hammer breaking open a turtle. Blood seeped from his nostrils. Tom had seen enough broken noses to know one when he saw it. Dull pain climbed up Tom's wrist and he hunched over, looking down at Donati's still body, hoping to God he hadn't killed him. A gentle wind made a hollow whisper as it sluiced between the beech trees on each side of the lonesome route, and Tom felt a deep sense of isolation, as if he was on a lost continent, an indifferent spot in a howling netherworld. He knelt down, took Donati's wrist and pressed his fingers to it.

There was a pulse.

Tom was able to breathe again. But there remained a great tension. This was assault and, because Tom had been a fighter, in the eyes of the law his hands were considered deadly weapons. This meant serious charges, and from the look of Donati, serious injuries. The blood had gone from trickling out of the man's nose to rolling down both sides of his face, and beneath his head, where he'd knocked his skull into the gravel, a red pool formed. The split in his lip revealed the tooth that had poked through the flesh. Tom watched the blood roll out from beneath the detective, unsure if he should try to move the man or not, if he should call it in or hightail it out of there. He found himself leaning toward the latter.

The guy's a scumbag. I think he and his friend caused that fire. He may be a private dick, but I'm thinking he's a criminal too. He won't file a complaint because he won't want to deal with the cops. He won't want to be questioned about the barn burning. Drag him further onto the shoulder, off the road, and leave. Pull his car off the road too and just leave the son of a bitch.

He glanced back and forth, half expecting the rotten luck of having another car appear, but the road remained empty, silent.

Even if he doesn't file a complaint, he'll want to get back at you for this. He might not come after you *either. He might try to get at you through Paige. He's already accosted her with little effort. How easy would it be for him to do something worse?*

There was little he could do about that. It wasn't like he could just kill the man. He didn't have that kind of violence in him. Tom wanted to stop Donati for good, to boot him out of their lives, but he wanted to do it the lawful way. If the situation were different he would have called the cops. That's what he should have done in the first place when he noticed Donati tailing him. Now it was too late. Calling Dale would get him in just as much trouble as Donati, more in fact.

The detective stirred, consciousness returning.

You've got to do something, man.

Tom waited, still crouched beside Donati. The detective's eyes fluttered. When he saw Tom he gasped and his hand raced into his coat. It happened so quickly that Tom didn't have time to process it.

He didn't realize that the man had a gun until it went off.

CHAPTER TWENTY-FOUR

The bullet whizzed by Tom's head, the shot so close it deafened his left ear. The worst headache he'd ever had rocked into his skull, jangling his brain like a can full of nickels. He fell backward but got to his feet as quick as he could. He headed toward his truck.

Maybe it was just a warning shot.

Another gunshot echoed through the valley, causing a murder of crows to rise from the treetops and sail into the falling snow. The bullet landed in the side of his truck, just a foot away from where he stood. Donati had gotten to his feet, but his legs were rubbery. His balance was thrown off after the mean hook Tom had given him, hindering his aim.

In the back of his truck was the hunting rifle. Tom figured it would take just as much time to grab it as it would to get the truck in gear and pull out, and if he did the latter he would still be getting shot at as he did so. He reached into the cab, pulling the rifle up, and spun around with it in both hands.

Donati was closing in, giving Tom no time to lock and aim. Instead he used the butt of the rifle as a battering ram, slamming Donati in the stomach as another round popped from his pistol and flew aimlessly through the air. Donati stumbled backward and Tom charged at him, both men stumbling across the road, over the shoulder, and then tumbling into the brush. They rolled down the incline and into the woods, spinning in the browned snow and crashing through yellow birch and bare bushes. Tom slammed into a tree with his back and dropped his rifle as pain exploded up his shoulders and neck. He heard Donati come to a stop too, so he got low to make himself a smaller target. He reached for his rifle.

Donati was lying in a heap of snow at the foot of a maple tree, his gun beside him on top of a small pool of ice. The man was motionless. One of his arms was bent up behind his head, still connected to his body but snapped off from the shoulder joint. Tom got to his feet, his aim on the man. Drawing closer, he realized Donati's head was facing the wrong way. Beneath the skin of his neck an array of bones jutted, making lumps in the flesh.

Oh, Jesus.

Tom lowered his rifle.

There was no reason to check the man's pulse this time.

Oh, holy Jesus.

Tom came back down to his knees, looking back and forth for nothing in particular. He was nearly hyperventilating, so he took long, deep breaths that made white puffs in the air.

The cars are still in the road.

Hurry.

He stood up, shaking.

You didn't do it. He fell.

But you pushed him, and before that you hit him.

He had gloves on, so he picked up Donati's pistol and opened the man's coat, placing it back into his shoulder holster.

I was never here.

It was snowing harder, hard enough to refill his footprints. Still he tried to walk through the area he'd fallen through to obscure it. He got up to the curb where the cars idled in the middle of road. There were still no other vehicles on the horizon. He moved fast, getting into Donati's car and pulling it over to the shoulder. Stepping out, he saw the blood that remained on the asphalt where Donati had dropped from Tom's punch. He went to his truck and reached into the cab, retrieving a can of wet wipes. He used every wipe left, sopping up the blood, then put them back into the can with a few pieces of stained gravel. He kicked the sand and rocks around to spread them out and reached into the snow bank and plopped a few handfuls over the spot, which was still a little red but no longer wet.

He noticed that he'd put tire streaks in the road when he'd hit his brakes.

Damn it!

He tossed the can of towels onto the passenger seat, moved his truck, and then got out again. Nervous energy was making his heart palpitate, and he sprinted to Donati's car. He backed it down the road and then headed for the tire tracks at full speed. The Town Car had good pickup, and he was going almost 50 when he slammed the brakes, somewhat obscuring the tracks his truck had made by road-burning the tires. He put the car back on the shoulder, but this time he backed it up several feet away from where the bloodstain had been.

All he could do now was hope.

He got into his truck and drove away, careful not to speed though he desperately wanted to. He turned the truck around and headed back toward Middlebury, wanting to show his face around town as much as possible now.

Tom ate at the diner, making small talk with Hannah and Russ. Then he stopped in the barbershop and got a long overdue cut. His left ear continued its high-pitched squeal now that his hearing had returned to it, and he tried not to use his busted right hand for anything. Tom stopped by Middlebury Tavern and had two beers to calm his rattled nerves and watched some other guys play pool, joking with them a little to get himself noticed.

I was nowhere near Route 12 today. Ask anybody.

When the time came he went to the bus stop. The snow had continued all afternoon and the roads were slushy and dangerous. The mother of the Godfrey boys was parked on the other side of the street. She waved to Tom and he waved back. Tom wondered if her husband had talked to the principal yet. He supposed he should follow up with him, but he had other things on his mind. Besides, there was no way Donati was going to show up at the school now. He wasn't going to show up anywhere but in that gulch.

He could have broken his nose in the fall.

That's what they'll think. Surely that's what they'll think.

He must have seen something from the road and went to investigate it. He must have slipped on some ice—a fatal accident, nothing more.

Tom still had a bullet hole in the side of his truck, but the truck was old and had a few rust spots on it already. He hoped it wasn't noticeable, that the discoloration of the truck would hide it. If someone looked closely they would notice, but without knowing it was there they would probably pass it right over. He wanted to believe that, but once he got home he would probably fiddle with it so it wouldn't look like a bullet hole. He could widen it or even plug it with something. He could weld a patch or put one of those metal stickers over it, a horse head or one of those naked ladies he always saw on mud flaps.

The bus roared in and Paige was the first one off.

They said hello.

Then they rode in silence.

CHAPTER TWENTY-FIVE

His name was not Donati.

Tom learned that the very next day.

It was Saturday, and Paige had an appointment with Dr. White first thing in the morning. Tom had a chat with the doctor alone, after Paige's session, to talk to her about Paige's infatuation with the alternate world she and Alice had created and discuss the dark nature of what she'd been writing, including the recreation of the murder.

White assured him that the recreation was totally normal, and that he'd been right to think it was just the child's way of processing what she'd seen. But the horror stories she'd been writing were another thing altogether. The focus on death and violence concerned White, but at the same time she agreed that addressing them would be a mistake at this point, because then Paige would know he had invaded her privacy, and that would have devastating after effects. White agreed to see Paige three times a week now, which made Tom feel better, but not much. Once again he was leaving her office with no answers.

Driving home, Tom rubbed his weary eyes. He hadn't been able to sleep last night. He kept replaying the scene with Donati, as if he was rewinding a movie clip over and over, hoping the videotape would finally wear out and rip. He heard the shot in his ear, felt the breeze of the bullet on his cheek. He felt his knuckles bend against the man's face and could smell the blood that bloomed around Donati's head like a comic book think-bubble. He felt the snow filling the back of his coat as he fell into the thicket, and whenever he closed his eyes the image of Donati's twisted carcass was projected onto the back of his eyelids.

But the man's name was not Donati.

The evening news told him so.

The body of former police officer Marty Gagliardi was found off of Route 12 early this morning… a trucker passing by noticed the car and stopped to help… an apparent accident… however, police are asking anyone with information…

Tom gulped, his mouth gone dry. *A former police officer?*

It made sense. A lot of private investigators had some law enforcement experience, didn't they? In all the pulp novels he'd read growing up, the P.I.s had usually been kicked off the force for boozing or playing by their own rules.

Dale is gonna put two and two together. Name aside, I told him a private eye was bugging us. He'll come calling about this soon enough. Just be ready. Hide your busted right hand. Remember, you were in town all afternoon. *Just because the guy was here to investigate you doesn't mean you had anything to do with his accident. There's no reason for anyone to jump to that conclusion.*

A thought suddenly jangled him like a slap to the face.

They'll check his gun.

They'll want to know if it was fired recently. Shit, if they look hard enough they might find the shell casings lying around.

He needed to cover up that bullet hole in his truck. Hopefully the snow would have covered up any of the shell casings at the scene. It had hammered down after he'd left, half an inch of snow dousing Coyote Valley before turning to sleet that turned the mounds into blocks of ice.

Would they be able to tell the gun was fired before taking it in for forensics? Would it still smell of gunpowder by then? Would they even bother searching the scene for shells in that case?

The snow had to melt sometime.

After dinner he went out to the utility shed and sifted through what he had. He was about to use a combination of duct tape and masking tape, but then he remembered he had some silicon calk. That stuff stuck to metal and stayed stuck. He pulled the truck into the garage and started off by making the hole as flat as he could with a hammer and dolly. Then he used the calk to fill it in. Luckily the truck was white, and the color of the calk was off-white—not exactly the same shade, but close enough to not be noticeable. It took a little while for him to get it smooth, but once he was finished he had to admit that it looked pretty good.

He turned at the sound of the door opening.

Paige stepped into the garage. "What're you doing?"

"Oh, just tinkerin, darlin."

"It's cold out here."

"Yeah, I guess it is. I'm almost done. What're you up to?"

She shrugged. "Nothing."

"There's gotta be somethin better to do than that."

She just stood there looking at him, and for a moment he was afraid that she knew he'd read her notebook, that she had purposely placed a single hair across it that he had unwittingly moved, giving away his intrusion.

If she did know, she didn't say anything about it.

He gathered his tools and told her to go back inside, that he just had to close up the utility shed. Stepping back out into the sorrow of the night, he looked at the black ruin of his barn in the middle of the pasture, crumpled there like a spent napkin. He thought of his herd and his horse tucked away in Fred's makeshift barn, and for a moment he felt like a mother who had just watched her grown child move out of the house. A sick, hollow feeling came over him, and he yearned for his wife and daughter.

Maybe they could have explained Paige to him.

~×~

Lying in bed that night, Tom started to doubt his choice to run. Had he called the police he could have said that Donati had come at him first, that Tom had just been defending himself, that they'd struggled and Donati had fallen to his death. But in the panic of the moment he hadn't thought of that. Now it was too late to call it in. He'd fled the scene of the crime. He was guilty and had to stick to his story and remember his alibis.

You had nothing to do with it, Tom.

When the house phone rang he jolted upright, his every nerve on edge. It was close to three a.m. and the jangle of the ringer went through him like he was sitting in the electric chair. He got out of bed and stepped into a pair of sweatpants. As he hurried downstairs, he wasn't surprised that the phone just kept on ringing. A call this late at night wouldn't be a casual one. The hour alone promised bad news.

Reaching the nightstand he waited in the dark, listening to the jingle-jangle. The receiver was cold when he picked it up.

"Who the hell is callin me at this hour?"

There was a wet clicking on the other end, a sniffle. Breath made static on the line.

"Who the hell is this?" Tom demanded. "Speak, ya sumbitch."

"So," the caller said. "I see dark sides run in the family."

The voice was female, slurred.

"Mrs. MacDougall?"

"Can the courtesy, Tommy. I think you can call me Fay after all we've been through together."

Tom's jaw tightened. "No, ma'am. I prefer Mrs. MacDougall."

She muttered something unintelligible.

"You can't be callin my house this late," he said. "In fact, I don't think you should be callin here at all."

"Let me ask you something, Tommy. Do you believe in angels?"

He knew he should hang up. *Hang up and unplug the phone.* But so much had happened already that he hoped he could talk some sense into the woman, drunk and grief-stricken though she may be. Perhaps he could reason with her and put an end to all of this.

"Well?" she asked. "Do you, Tommy? Do you believe in angels?"

He couldn't help but think of Betty. "I suppose I do, in a way. There are livin angels on Earth, anyhow."

"Ahhh. That's exactly what I'm talking about here. Earth-fucking-angels. That's what my baby was. My Alice. She was an Earth angel." She sniffled again. "She didn't deserve what happened to her. To die like that... in the woods... like an animal. She didn't deserve that."

"Well, ma'am, that's one thing we can certainly agree on."

"See? I knew you'd understand. I tried to tell my brother. I told him you were a decent man. Everybody in town knows that."

"Maybe you could tell your brother again. Get all these bans on my ranch lifted and keep his detectives outta my life."

"Looks like one of them's already gone."

He didn't reply.

"My brother is a very intense individual when he wants something, Tommy. He won't back down at all."

"And just what does he want from me?"

"The same thing I want: the truth."

"Now I've done told you and told you again. You got the truth—all of it."

"From you. But not from her."

Tom felt the heat rising in him and he took a moment to collect himself.

"Mrs. MacDougall, I feel for you here, truly and deeply. But I'm tellin you, if you keep thinkin the way you are, ain't either of us gonna find peace."

More silence from her, then: "Let me ask you another question. How far would you go if it was your little daughter?"

His mind threw an image at him: Dawn, when she was ten, twirling in the summer sunshine with their golden retriever Sunday yapping at her heels. Now ol' Sunday was buried under the sycamore that hung over the ranch like a withered umbrella, and Dawn was buried beside her husband in a cemetery in Massachusetts where the sun shone down unobstructed, feeding the flowers around it.

"There's nowhere else to go," he told her. "It's in the police's hands. Leave it there."

"They don't know what I know! They won't listen to me when I try to tell them that that Paige of yours is a rotten apple! Alice told me about their little stories, you know. She told me how Paige started scaring her with all her made-up monsters. All that blood and gore. There's darkness inside that little girl! She's a bad seed!"

"I'm not gonna listen to this."

"You know it's true! Tell me you haven't had the same thoughts!"

"Goodnight, Mrs. MacDougall."

As he hung up the phone he heard her shouting one last thing.

Tom told himself he'd heard her wrong and that she couldn't have said what he'd thought she'd said.

He wanted to believe that.

He unplugged the phone when it began to ring again. As he climbed up the stairs, he saw that Paige was standing at the railing, looking down at him. She'd been listening. They locked eyes, but he didn't know what to say to her anymore.

Paige looked down at him with no expression.

She asked him no questions, said nothing at all.

Turning around, she walked back into the darkness of her room.

CHAPTER TWENTY-SIX

It was a warmer day. Tom had barely slept a wink, but there were chores to do. He guzzled several cups of coffee and filled his belly with a BLT. Paige had a bowl of cereal and was eating it in front of the TV, watching *SpongeBob SquarePants*, a show Tom couldn't wrap his mind around.

"I'm going down to Mr. Hollister's to get the cattle movin," he told her. "I want you to stay in the house while I'm gone."

"Okay."

He made sure to lock the door behind him when he left and decided to bring his rifle with him, the events of the week keeping him on guard. He slung the rifle over his shoulder and zipped up his coat, appreciating the mellow nature of the day. If only the sun would come out, he just might find a reason to smile.

He started down the driveway, and as he reached the curb he saw a cruiser heading toward him. He stood tall and waited, knowing that at this point it could be anything.

He was glad the truck was still in the garage and that he had gloves on.

Parking the car, Dale stepped out, looking even more tired and deflated than Tom felt. The man's eyes were hollowed out behind his glasses and he appeared aged by the natural light. They said their good mornings and Dale got down to it.

"Suppose you heard about that accident on Friday?"

Sweat beaded at the base of Tom's lower spine. He put his hands in his pockets to hide their trembling.

"Reckon I did."

"Did you know it was that private eye fellar?"

Tom went wide-eyed, playing dumb. "Donati? That was him?"

Dale nodded. "Ayuh."

"Shoot. I just thought they said it was some old cop. Had some other name, right?"

"Gagliardi was his real name. When workin he went by Donati for the sake of his own privacy. He was an ex-cop, and a crooked one at that. Got kicked offa the force back in '99."

"News folk said he slipped on ice or somethin, right? Fell into the woods?"

"Found him up against a tree with his neck broke from a fall."

Tom whistled with a pained face. "Well, goddamn."

"I just wanted to know if he'd been around you or Paige any since we last spoke, or if you'd heard from him at all."

Tom took a moment to act like he was thinking about it. "No, last we saw him was when he accosted Paige at the school."

Dale rubbed his chin, making Tom's blood pump his heart, tequila spat on a bonfire.

"Thing is," Dale began, "I just can't rightly figure what the man was doin out on Route 12, not too far from your ranch at all."

Tom shrugged. "Must've been spyin again. Them people just won't leave us alone, Dale. In fact, Mrs. MacDougall called me last night. Woke us up at three in mornin."

"Really, now?"

"Ayuh." Tom was happy to have changed the subject.

"What'd she want?" Dale asked.

"She said the same thing she was sayin at the funeral, only louder and meaner, with worse implications."

Dale shook his head. "That's another little problem we've got there, that Fay MacDougall. She's been causin trouble all over town."

"Oh?"

"She ain't been right since her baby died. Can't say I blame her, but she's been drinkin hard and carryin on, bein nasty to anybody that so much as glances at her. Her husband's had a helluva time lookin after her, I can tell ya. Even now he don't know where she is. Called in askin us to look for her."

"She missin?"

"Not officially. She just took off in the car last night and ain't been back. He's worried about her mental state. Says she's always drunk and don't sleep much no more. I've spoken with them about you, and spoke to Mr. Sands, and warned them about harassment. You want me to pay her another visit once she comes back home, talk to her about this phone call?"

"Nah, I guess not. She was plenty drunk. She's just a sad woman. I feel bad for her."

"We all do, but that don't give her free reign to bother you or anybody else that way." Dale looked out to the snowy crest, his shoulders sagging but his eyes hardening like a block of ice. "You know, the men in my family, it's always been our jobs to keep this land civilized. Either I'm gettin old, or it's a lot harder than it used to be." His breath made a wisp in the air. "I'll talk to her. You take care, Tom, and take care of that lil girl."

"I will."

As Dale turned to his cruiser he took one more look at Tom. "Plannin on doin some huntin today?"

It took Tom a moment to remember he had the rifle strapped to his back. He figured he'd lied to his friend enough for one day.

"Not really," he said.

Dale merely nodded and got back into the car, waving as he headed out through the slush, idling along toward Route 12.

~

Essie seemed happy to be out and moving. She'd been taken care of by the vet and was ready for exercise. She was riding easy but galloped with enthusiasm, and Tom found himself enjoying being on horseback and wrangling the herd. The work was taking his mind off of things and letting him get back to the core of his existence, what he was meant to do, what he was meant to be. The cowboy life grounded and empowered him. Even when the work was grueling and the land was unforgiving, Tom still found rejuvenation in doing what he did. It was a job he was proud of, the only thing that gave him the satisfaction boxing had when he was a much younger man.

Over the bluff the livestock roamed, ready to graze and defecate. The sky was white, reflecting the snowy earth, and the only sound was that of the hooves crunching the snow and the occasional lowing of the animals that encircled him like a wreath. With the summit cleared, they wrestled their way onto the ranch, coming around the side of the house and into the clearing. A breeze had picked up and beyond the hillside the dead trees rocked like metronomes, their arms burdened by snow.

When he first saw movement he thought it was the thicket itself, but the shapes moved fluidly, alive.

Deer? Coyotes?

He clucked to Essie and headed toward the tree line, squinting. He could only make out a small, dark blob at first. But then she stood up and he knew it was Paige. She was building a snowman.

He was agitated that she had left the house despite his explicit instructions, but that thought quickly passed when another movement flashed, a flutter of white coming into view.

Tom stopped breathing.

Paige was not alone.

CHAPTER TWENTY-SEVEN

Paige seemed totally unaware of the woman in white.

The woman moved slowly, walking up behind the child, looking like a poltergeist with her pale skin and housedress. She was terribly underdressed for the snowy day, with no coat, hat or gloves. Her hair was in disarray, a blonde hurricane, and she was having trouble trenching through the snow. Looking at her legs, Tom saw that she was barefoot. Her face was flushed, but recognizable.

Fay MacDougall.

They were too far away to hear him shout. He kicked Essie's ribs and the horse galloped, snow exploding around them. Fay was drawing closer to Paige's turned back, and there was something in her hand, something that gleamed.

"Hey!" he shouted. "Hey!"

Tom was gaining ground now, and this time they heard him. Paige turned his way but Fay kept walking toward her, the knife rising higher. The girl spotted her now, got up, and took a step back.

"Run, Paige!" Tom cried.

But the girl was frozen. She seemed only able to back up one step at a time.

"Run! Run!"

He was closer, but still not close enough, and Fay was closing in on his granddaughter. He could see her face now, pale and dead, the face of a woman in a vegetated state, the eyes of a vampire.

"Fay! Stop!"

She briefly looked at him before turning back to Paige, her objective clear. Tom got as close as he had time to, then reined Essie to a halt and pulled at the strap of the rifle, slinging it off in one swift movement. The barrel came up, he closed one eye, and as he zeroed in on Fay he saw that she was nearly on top of Paige now. The girl stood frozen, looking up at Fay with the lifeless face of a china doll, as if waiting for the blade to pierce her heart.

A deafening crack echoed through the valley.

Birds bailed out of their hiding spots as the top of Fay MacDougall's head came off, bits of skull bursting and scattering, blood misting the air like spray paint. Her head snapped back and her legs failed, sending her crashing to her knees. She toppled over backward and crumpled like a pile of rags. The snow turned pink beneath her, a slowly opening rose.

Tom dismounted and ran to the woman's body. Blood was pouring out of both nostrils in a horrible rush, thick and purple and grotesque. The top of her head was ripped clean off and flakes of skull were meshed with her seeping grey matter. Her eyes stared up at him, empty, glass. One whole side of her forehead was gone.

Tom held a hand to his mouth, letting the rifle fall beside him. The hot barrel hissed in the frost as Paige stepped forward, staring down at the body.

Tom tried to turn her away. "Don't look, darlin."

His mind was racing as quickly his heart. The world around them seemed to tighten and condense, and there was a terrible stillness to it now—quiet, detached. Paige stepped in, seeming just as detached from the scene, a look of bored apathy on her face.

Was she dazed?

Coldness spread through Tom like white noise as he saw the lack of emotion in the little girl's face. There was no fear, sadness or confusion. Her hands did not shake as his did. Only her hair moved, blowing gently in the wind, flitting like black leaves.

He remembered what Fay had been saying last night as he'd hung up the phone, and now he knew that he'd heard her correctly.

She killed my daughter, the woman had said.

CHAPTER TWENTY-EIGHT

Once again, a fleet of police vehicles surrounded the ranch. Officers roped it off with yellow tape while the medical crew covered Fay's body, declaring her dead at the scene. Tom watched them from afar, sitting on his front stoop. A cup of coffee he struggled to hold steady was warming his hands. The swirling lights made the snow dunes flicker red, reminding him of all the blood he'd seen and shed in just a few days. His stomach was hollowed by it, his soul aching like a fresh wound.

They'd found Fay MacDougall's car down the street. She'd hit a tree but hadn't been going that fast. Only the front bumper was dented, but the tires were sunk deep into the snow. Empty bottles of wine littered the floorboards. The knife she carried was a sturdy buck-hunting knife, likely a possession of her husband's.

Tom answered all the questions. Everything was cut and dry and nobody seemed to disbelieve him. There were no suspicious glances, only ones of pity. It seemed like the entire police force was out there now. Tom wondered how long it would take for word of this to get to town, if it hadn't already. What would happen when word reached Sands? Tom thought of Troy MacDougall, a nice man who'd now lost his wife as well as his daughter. He thought of the shadow this cast and how it would follow him for the rest of his life, and how Paige would forever be cloaked by that shadow as long as she lived in Middlebury. This town had already labeled her a black sheep, a weirdo. Now she would be even further ostracized.

The girl was inside now, having spoken to the police already. Tom made her some cocoa and put on cartoons for her. He hoped they would bring her comfort, however small. Tom doubted they were powerful enough to clean the fresh memories of murder in her head. He wondered if anything ever could.

She's traumatized. That's why she's been so lifeless. She can't handle this. Hell, neither can I.

"I should have known this was comin," Dale said.

"Me too."

"Poor woman was comin unraveled. She got it in her head that Paige was somehow responsible for us not bein able to catch the killer, and that thought stuck in her head until it drove her plumb crazy."

They stood side by side, watching the paramedics load Fay into the back of the ambulance. Flurries frenzied against the sky, making the scene seem even more dreamlike, surreal.

"There's no stoppin what's done," Tom said. "But what's not done yet is somethin different."

"I hear ya, friend. I hear ya."

"Think I have any more to worry about?"

Dale removed his glasses and rubbed his eyes. "I just don't know anymore. Every time I think I know this town, the people surprise me in the worst ways."

"Sands already sicked his goons on me and shut down a good deal of my business. Might've even had someone burn down my barn. I hate to think what he's gonna do now."

"He hired investigators. There's no law against that. As far as the fire department is concerned, the barn was spontaneous combustion. And I can't stop Sands from screwin you over business-wise."

"He likes to push, and he's got the money to push pretty damn hard. That makes me worry. I don't know what the man's capable of."

Dale looked up at the icicles that hung above them, then out to the rolling hills of white. "I'd like to think that maybe this is the end of it all. I must admit that I've all but lost hope when it comes to findin Alice's killer. We won't give up, but my heart is sick with the feelin that we're just gonna keep turnin up empty. But I do hope that this is the last time I'll have to be out your way for somethin other than a friendly hello."

Tom shook his head. "Well, I've made up my mind already."

"About what?"

"About this place. There ain't no stayin here now, not after all that's happened. I might be able to carry on, but Paige won't be able to recover from this with all these people around to remind her. She already gets teased at school. I reckon now she'll be downright tortured."

"Thinkin of sellin the ranch then?"

"Shit, Dale, I'm already lookin at spendin thousands on a new barn, ain't I? I figure why not cut my losses and head somewhere new? Maybe out west, see some canyons. There's too many ghosts here now, and I'm too old to chase em all away. All I can do is try to lose em in the dust." He took a deep breath, releasing it in a slow, long exhale. "More than anythin, I don't want em hauntin Paige. I'm her guardian; I owe it to her, and to my daughter Dawn, to give her a decent life if not an altogether good one. This valley has nothin left for her but pain and lots of it."

The men stood in silence then. A bit of sleet meshed with the flurries, clacking on the roofs of cars and bouncing away like fleas. The ambulance skidded on the snowy shoulder and righted itself in the road, and Tom and Dale watched it carry Fay MacDougall—the second person Tom had killed in just three days—away from the ranch, away from the valley, and away from the land of the living, forever.

PART FOUR

THE HEART OF A CHILD

CHAPTER TWENTY-NINE

Tom was going to flat out ask Mary for help. He didn't know who else he could reach out to. She was the closest thing to family that he had left.

He looked out the window as he clutched the phone, listening to it ring. He'd been watching the windows steadily over the past two days and had kept Paige home from school. He was filled with distrust and deep concern. Dale might not think that Sands or the MacDougalls would retaliate for Fay's death, but Tom had a nagging hunch that revenge was brewing. Now that Tom had killed Sands's sister, there was no telling what the man might do, or pay someone else to do. Tom doubted the fact that he'd only been protecting his granddaughter would factor into Sands's reasoning.

"Hello, Mary."

He told her all that had happened since they'd last spoke, with the exception of what he'd done to Donati. She was silent at first. She began to sniffle and Tom's heart swelled at her empathy. She was a good and kind woman.

"I don't feel like we're safe anymore," he said. "I've got this feelin that somethin mean is comin. Trouble's so thick in the air I can almost smell it."

"What are you going to do?"

"I dunno. I've got a ranch to keep up and I've gotta start movin some meat to keep the money rollin in. I need to make new connections. Now, I can handle myself and what might be comin. It's Paige I'm worried about. I'd like to get her away from here, at least for a little while. I was thinking, maybe..."

"Oh," she said. "Oh, Tom, I'm sorry but—"

"Just for a few days until I can figure this out. It'll give me time to see if Sands or his goons pull anythin. I'll also get a lot more business done without havin to keep an eye on her all day."

"Tom, I'm so sorry, but we just can't. David hasn't been well and my knees have gone bad. I'm just getting too old to keep up with a little girl."

"She's ten, she's mostly self-sufficient."

"You just said how hard it is to get things done while keeping an eye on her."

"I guess I did. I'm sorry, Mary. I don't mean to impose on y'all. I know David's been strugglin with the diabetes. I just had to ask, you know?"

She sighed. "Is there anything else I can do to help? Could I send you some money?"

"No, no. Come on now."

"I just thought maybe the two of you could get away together for a little while until this blows over."

"I don't know if somethin like this ever really blows over. But I see what you mean."

"Couldn't you hire someone to take care of the livestock until you come back?"

It was a thought.

"They're at the Hollister's," Tom said, "and Willard knows how to handle em. He was raised a farmer but he's been bull ridin and doin rodeos for years. He's good with em. I might be able to hire him as a hand for a few days, considerin."

"I think that's a great idea. Take Paige on a vacation. Get her away from all of this."

"Just wish it wasn't winter. Most fun things are closed. I'd have to take her all the way down to Orlando for theme parks, and I just can't afford to do that. Not that I'd ever want to set foot in that awful state again."

Mary chuckled. Tom had a reputation for hating swamps and beaches, and that was all Florida had to offer. He'd taken Betty there for vacation once and had complained about the humidity and mosquitoes to no end.

"I'm sure there's museums or landmarks you could visit. Would she like that?"

"Maybe. I have trouble knowin what she likes and doesn't. Seems like every day she's harder to read."

"This is a lot for a child to handle."

"Ayuh."

"It can't be very easy for you either. My heart goes out to you and I really do wish I could be of more help."

"Just talkin to ya helps, Mary. I appreciate it."

❥

"But where are we gonna go?" Paige asked.

"We'll see."

"*We'll see?*"

"It's fun to hit the open road and just go wherever our hearts desire. We'll take a little road trip, see some sights and stay at hotels. I'll find one with indoor heated pools so you can go swimmin. Sound good?"

"It sounds like we'll just be driving around." Her voice was flat and emotionless, her eyes revealing premature boredom.

"It'll be more than that. Besides, it'll give us plenty of time to talk. We can get to know each other better. I'd like that. Hope you would too."

"But what about school? I'll get behind."

"You'll be back soon enough."

"But—"

"Enough buts! I want us to hit the road, so pack your things because we're goin. Case closed."

———

In the days leading up to their road trip, Tom kept Paige home from school, and other than doctor visits, they stayed out of town. They'd been visiting Dr. White every day since the incident with Fay. But the psychologist had little answers, just words of encouragement and suggestions of patience and understanding. She liked the idea of them taking a vacation, but warned him that Paige didn't want to go, as if he didn't know already.

———

Willard agreed to handle the livestock while they were gone. Tom promised him fifteen bucks an hour for his trouble, took one last round of the livestock, and gave Essie a new salt lick before leaving the herd in Willard's hands.

That night they packed with plans to leave in the morning.

They sat in the living room, Tom watching TV while Paige colored. He wasn't able to pay attention, though. He was filled with jarring mental images of Fay's head coming apart, making him wince and shudder.

He was a murderer.

Sure, Donati was an accident, and Fay was certainly justifiable, but that didn't change the way he felt. It was even worse than it had been when he'd come back from the war. He felt as if there was a taint on his very soul, a black stain that bubbled and festered like used motor oil. And he just couldn't stop thinking about the killings.

It surprised him when he saw Christmas commercials on the television. He thought about mentioning it to Paige, that it might cheer her up, but he'd failed to excite her with the holidays before, and after all that had happened he doubted she'd feel anymore jovial about them. She hadn't mentioned Christmas at all.

A ten-year-old girl and she hasn't mentioned Christmas.

His heart would break over that if it weren't already shattered.

Outside, there was a wet crackle of tires on the snow-dusted road. Tom turned to the window to watch the car go by, relief washing over him when the headlights disappeared. He watched the road closely now, always pausing what he was doing to make sure no one stopped near the ranch. He kept the rifle locked and loaded, and he'd unearthed his old .38 snub-nose from the bowels of the closet, cleaned and loaded it. It was transferred from room to room with him, and he made sure Paige didn't see when he tucked it into jeans or hid it in the drawers of end tables. He told himself he was getting paranoid, but that didn't stop him from carrying the gun around.

"Grandpa?" Paige called, dragging him out of the darkness of his thoughts.

"Yes, darlin?"

She looked at her drawing, searching for words with a furrowed brow. "I just want you to know… you did the right thing."

Tom blinked. "How's that?"

"With Mrs. MacDougall."

He gulped hard and shifted in his seat. "I know, darlin."

"She was a bad woman, wasn't she?"

"Well, I think she was a *sick* woman."

"Sick? Like, with the flu?"

"No, I mean up here." He pointed to his head. "People can get sick in the brain. It's like any other organ. Your heart can fail, your kidneys, your liver. The brain can too. And when it does it makes you think things that don't make sense, makes you believe things that ain't true, and sometimes it makes you act on those things in ways you never would normally."

"So she was crazy?"

"Mentally ill, yes."

Paige studied him now. "You mean like me?"

Tom leaned forward. "No, darlin. Not like you."

"But I'm mentally ill, aren't I, Grandpa? That's why you take me to Dr. White. She's not a regular doctor. She's a crazy person doctor."

She didn't seem upset now, whereas before she had been adamant about objecting to the notion of her being emotionally troubled. She seemed very straightforward, as if trying to get him to accept a harsh reality she'd already come to terms with.

"No, she isn't a crazy person doctor," he said. "She's a doctor that helps people get through hard times. You've been through a lot of em lately—more than any lil girl should ever have to."

"That's why I'm crazy then? Because of all of this stuff that's happened?"

"You're not crazy, honey."

"Well, Mom and Dad thought so."

He paused. "What?"

"Mom and Dad. They took me to see a brain doctor too, and that was before all of this happened. They thought I was crazy and so do you. So does everybody."

Tom sat upright. He'd never known anything about Dawn taking Paige for psychiatric care before. And he felt sure that if Betty had known she would have told him.

"Why didn't you mention this before, about your mama takin you to see a psychiatrist?"

She shrugged. "I dunno."

"Look, I don't think you're crazy and neither did your folks. Sometimes people just need a little help with their emotions."

"But some people get head sick and do crazy things. That's what you just said. They're not having a problem with emotions. Their brain is mixed up. That's what you said."

He took her hand between his. It felt so small, so cold. "You're not like that, Paige."

Her eyes were lost. "But... what if I am?"

There was no concern in her eyes. Only challenge.

"You're... not..." He started a sentence he had no finish for.

Paige stood up and went to the window, draping her arms on the sill and resting her chin on her hands. "I don't feel crazy. But if you're crazy, how would you know? I think it's the others who are crazy. They think they're all so important. They think nothing bad can ever happen and they're never gonna die. But there are dark things out there, even if they can't see them. And they do what they want. They take parents. They take princes and princesses. They take little girls."

Tom put his chin in his hand. He had no words to counter hers—none at all. He didn't like what raced through his head, so he clenched

129

his teeth upon a knuckle to fight against the thoughts.

Suddenly white light moved across the room.

It came from outside, pushing through the window. Tom turned to look, seeing the same car that had passed the house earlier coming back from the other direction. It pulled into the driveway, making no effort to hide.

Tom shot up. "Go to your room—*now*."

"But I didn't do anything."

"You ain't punished, I just need you to go to your room."

She picked up her paper and crayons and huffed toward the stairs. Once she was out of sight, Tom took the pistol from the end table's drawer. He headed for the door and watched through the window as a man got out of the car and started toward the house. He was dressed in a suit and tie, a heavy trench coat covering him. He didn't look like some bodybuilder, as Fred had described Donati's sidekick. He was of average size with spectacles and a clean look about him. Very nonthreatening, but Tom didn't trust the trench coat. It could be concealing anything. He kept the gun in hand, hiding it behind the door as he opened it halfway.

The man smiled at him as he approached the porch. He was carrying a manila envelope.

"Hello. Mr. Hargrave?"

"Ayuh."

When the man reached the door he extended a hand that Tom didn't shake. The man dropped his arm with a small frown, but the smile quickly returned, ironed on like a salesman's.

"I'm Gary Orenstein of Morgan, Morgan and Sloan. We represent Mr. Gerald Sands."

"You're a lawyer?"

"Well, I work for the firm."

"Okay, so you represent Sands. What're you representin him for that concerns me?"

Orenstein handed him the envelope. Tom turned it over and popped it open. With some difficulty, he pulled out a thick stack of papers, all very official looking with seals and dense text.

"Mr. Sands is filing civil charges against you," Orenstein said, "for the wrongful death of his sister Fay MacDougall and her daughter Alice MacDougall. Everything you need to know is in the folder."

Tom flushed. "Civil charges? The police already ruled on both of these here incidents. He can't file no charges against me."

"Actually he can, sir, and he has."

"He's tryin to hold me responsible for what happened to his sister and niece? How can he do that? Fay's death was in defense of my granddaughter, and I had nothin to do with Alice's death."

"You are the guardian of the girl who was with Alice at the time of her murder. Mr. Sands is filing suit. The complaint is in and I advise you to seek an attorney and have them contact us once they have the paperwork."

Tom looked at the papers again. Technical jargon glared up at him mockingly.

"Good day to you, Mr. Hargrave."

Orenstein turned and walked down the driveway, stepping carefully through the patches of ice.

"Tell that son of a bitch he's wastin his time and his money!" Tom shouted. "Tell him Tom Hargrave has had enough of his bullshit! If he wants to make trouble, I hope he'll stretch first, 'cause I promise him a good fight. You tell him that!"

The man waved but didn't turn back or reply.

Tom slammed the door.

CHAPTER THIRTY

He had thirty days to respond to the court, but this prevented them leaving town now. He had to get himself an attorney to go over the paperwork and help him build a defense. The suit was frivolous, enacted just to make life difficult for Tom. Gerald Sands wanted to tie him up and make him spend money he didn't have. Sands certainly had plenty of cash to feed his legal attack dogs, even if he had no chance of winning the case. If he did, Tom's savings could be cleaned out and his wages garnished for a long time to come.

Sands can't really think he'll win can he?

It seemed too preposterous.

Maybe Sands didn't want to just take up his time and money, but also to publicly shame Tom by further associating him with the MacDougall killings. Even if he wasn't found guilty, his friends and neighbors would always be reminded of the case that had been made against him. It would leave a permanent scar on his good name, making it harder for him to market his ranch.

So win or lose the case, Tom was still going to lose.

He decided to let Willard handle his herd for a while even though they'd be staying in town. He needed the break to get his affairs in order and more importantly get his head straight. His thoughts were muddied and racing, his emotions getting the better of him.

Evening fell heavy as a storm, the early darkness depressed and fully enveloped. Tom made a simple dinner of chicken cutlets and canned peas, his mind and heart not involved in what he was doing. Paige had to remind him to add butter to the peas, but she set the table like a good girl and poured each of them a glass of milk.

Tom hadn't wanted a drink this badly since he'd quit. A Jack and a beer back had always been his poison, and he was trying to convince himself that just one wouldn't hurt, that he needed it now and even deserved it for being so good about not drinking for so long. But that was a nasty, trickster ghoul of a voice he knew all too well. As it nagged, he tried to ignore it through dinner, and even though he couldn't block it out completely, he wasn't about to run to the liquor store. Even if he lost control enough to head out there he knew he'd never make it. Thoughts of Betty and his promise would be a roadblock, and he'd end up turning the truck around and coming home.

"I can't stand for this no more, Tom," she had said on that day, all those years ago. "If you get a D.U.I. it's the last straw, you hear me? Bad enough that the kids see you stumblin all over the house, but now you're puttin people in danger by drivin home from the bar sauced."

Tom had sneered. "I work hard. I have a right to relax."

"You can relax all you want if I leave and take the kids with me. Maybe then you'll finally understand I'm serious. Lord knows you've ignored me up to this point."

And that's what it had taken. When he refused to quit drinking, Betty had gone off to Mary's house with their children, vowing not to return until he sacrificed his drinking habit. It had scared Tom so badly that he'd quit cold turkey. He relapsed a time or two after Betty came back, but she stuck by him, helping him overcome his addiction. They'd beaten it together, but the process had tainted his family life. His children's opinion of him had slid down a dark curve, never to return to the high spot it had once held.

Best to just stay in with his granddaughter now. Enough horror had befallen them without him falling back into his oldest one by hitting the bourbon.

At Paige's bedtime he said goodnight and she went to her room without fuss, but later, when he passed by on his way to the bathroom, he noticed a small touch of light under her door.

She's using a flashlight, probably to write in her notebook.

Tom let her be, hoping she could work out her dark thoughts in her little book. He was still jarred by all that she'd said. It filled him with bad ideas.

Why had Dawn taken her to a psychiatrist? Did Paige have a condition or was she just struggling emotionally? Why hadn't Dawn ever mentioned it to Tom or Betty? Was she ashamed?

The thoughts were too dark for him to face head-on, so he tried to turn away from them all together.

Back downstairs, he tried to unwind with an old western movie, but his mind continued to roam. The dominoes that had fallen after Alice's murder had mounted to a staggering pinnacle, each one striking towards the next until the entire row would collapse. He ached for a rewind button on life, so he could go back to right before Alice had been killed and join the girls in the woods, prevent the murder, or at least see for himself what had really happened.

⌐⌐

Jep woke him.

The dog always slept at the foot of the bed, and he was roused now, making small barks and growling.

"What, boy?"

Tom heard footfalls downstairs.

Paige?

He got out of bed and stepped into his sweatpants. Jep knew better than he did if it was the girl, and judging by the dog's growls, this was someone else, someone who did not belong here.

Damn it!

He'd forgotten the .38. It was still downstairs. He tried to think of something else he could use as a weapon. Looking around the room he saw the metal elephant statue Betty had bought some years back at a crafts fair. He snatched it and held it over his shoulder as he inched out the door.

"Heel," he whispered to Jep to keep the dog from charging downstairs.

Jep moved alongside of him, his hackles raised, a rumbling in his throat. Together they headed to the railing that overlooked the living room and front foyer. Tom didn't see anything, and the end table was right there, the drawer with the pistol in it calling to him. The kitchen was adjacent to the living room, so he walked down the stairs slowly, watching the open doorway.

A big, ominous shadow moved past, a monster from a child's nightmare. He hoped Paige was still asleep in her room, the door locked. Tom's breath caught in his chest and, sensing his nervousness, Jep growled louder. The shadow turned. Tom couldn't see the man's face but knew the man had spotted them. His huge silhouette loomed.

"Who the hell's that?" Tom asked.

Slowly, the man kept coming. As he stepped past the foyer the light of the moon hit him, revealing a muscular body and a pockmarked face.

It's the big guy, Tom thought, *Donati's sidekick.*

"Mr. Hargrave, I'm Andre," the man said. "At last we meet."

"What're you doin here? How'd you get into my house?"

"You should invest in a more serious lock for your back door."

"Worked fine until you got here. State your business. You're Donati's buddy, ain't ya?"

"Something like that."

"You're the one who was snoopin round my barn."

The man was close now, but not close enough for Tom to whack him with the elephant. Tom saw that he was unarmed but figured there must be something in his coat. If not, his body was a weapon in and of itself.

"I was investigating. That's all. Marty and I had nothing to do with the fire. We were sorry to hear about that."

"Like hell."

"It's true. I don't know why you think we were such bastards. We were just performing an investigation."

"Well he berated my granddaughter and you drove his getaway car."

"That's true. I advised Marty against that. It was just a spur of the moment error."

"Like breakin in here?"

"Oh, there's no error in that." Now the man reached into his coat and drew out a 9mm. "See, I know what Marty was doing on the day he died. He had me on speakerphone while he was tailing you. I thought about letting the police know, but came to a different solution. One that pleased me much more."

Jep barked at the man's threat.

"I like dogs," Andre said. "But I'll put a bullet in this one if you don't curb him."

Tom pushed Jep behind his legs.

Andre leaned in. "Now drop that little statue."

Tom did as he was told. "Listen, Donati—Marty, I mean—was an accident."

"Is that so?"

"I caught him tailin me and we had an argument. We got into a shovin match and we fell down the slope together. He hit a tree and that was that. He died instantly. There was nothin I could do to help him, otherwise I woulda."

"An accident."

"Ayuh."

"One hell of an accident."

"That it was."

"Well, old man, it looks like you're going to have an accident of your own."

Andre reeled back to pistol-whip him, but Tom had good reflexes from his boxing years and managed to pull his head out of range. The big man fell off balance as he missed, tumbling toward Tom, and seeing the opening Tom punched him right in his liver and followed it up with a left hook to the jaw. Andre's body felt like granite, but he crumbled, grabbing Tom by the legs and pulling at his calves, making him fall backward against the bottom of the stairs. Jep ran around them, barking like crazy. Tom tried to kick at Andre but his knees were weak and he moved too slowly. The man caught his foot and tried to punch him in the balls but missed, hitting his upper thigh. Tom rolled away from him, trying to reach the elephant. Then he felt the cold touch of the gun barrel hit the back of his neck.

"Now just settle down," Andre said.

There were footsteps upstairs.

A door opened.

"Who's that?" Andre asked.

Tom didn't want to say.

"Grandpa?" Paige asked from the hall above, still out of sight.

"Tell her to go back to bed," Andre whispered.

"Sorry, honey," Tom called to the balcony. "I just banged into something. Go back to sleep."

She didn't reply but Tom could hear her footsteps. He wasn't sure if she was coming closer or going back to her room.

"Please," he whispered. "It's just my granddaughter."

"I gathered."

"She's just a little girl. Please, don't harm her."

"I'm not a monster, Hargrave. It's only you I came for."

Tom was relieved to hear it, but shuddered at the sound of tiny footfalls on the stairs.

"What's going on?" she asked, her shadow coming into view.

Tom felt the 9mm leave his neck and Andre's hands went into his armpits to help him up. He walked them into the kitchen, hiding behind the wall but leaving Tom in the doorway, the gun aimed at him. The big man nodded, telling Tom all he needed to know.

"Nothin, baby," Tom said. "Everythin's fine."

Paige moved toward him. "I thought I heard you talking to someone."

"Oh, just talkin to Jep."

The dog's attention was locked on to Andre, his hackles still raised although he had fallen silent.

"But I heard another man," Paige said.

"No, just me. Maybe you were dreamin."

Her little face pinched. "I wasn't *dreamin* and I don't believe you. Someone's in the kitchen, aren't they?"

"Go upstairs!" he said. "Get up there right now or you're grounded."

That got her. Her face went sour, a pale mask in the moonlight. "What did I do?"

"Don't ask questions, just do as I tell ya."

She gave him a strange and curious look, but backed up and turned toward the stairs, taking them two at a time as she huffed her way up. Once she rounded the corner to the hall, Tom retreated into the kitchen.

"Thank you," he said to Andre.

"Don't thank me yet."

"Look, can we just talk about this for a minute?"

"You wanna talk? Okay, go ahead and talk."

"Well, I just wanna say this won't help matters none. I'm tellin you straight that Marty was an accident. I mean, I had no reason to want to kill him, did I?"

The man remained silent, cloaked in shadow.

"Hell," Tom said. "What's this gonna solve? You don't want a killin hangin over your head, do ya? Especially of an old man who has a little girl to take care of. I can see you're a better man than that by how you let me keep her outta this. You don't want her to find my body and then end up in some orphanage, do ya?"

The refrigerator thrummed, surrounding them in rattling, white noise. Finally, Andre spoke.

"Marty was my *partner*, Mr. Hargrave—"

"I understand, but—"

"No, you *don't* understand. He wasn't just my partner as detectives. He was my *life partner*. Now maybe you understand."

Tom's eyes widened. *Gay? These two?* They certainly didn't match up with his idea of the type. They both seemed as straight as a ruler, and Andre was at least twenty years younger than Donati.

Then again, maybe I think in old-fashioned stereotypes when it comes to homosexuals.

"I'm sorry," Tom said. "Really, I am. I lost my wife not too long ago. So yeah, I do understand."

Tom heard a sniffle in the dark and he turned toward it, seeing that Andre's hands were by his sides now, the pistol lowered.

Andre's voice was a croak. "He didn't deserve to die like that."

"I know." It was the second time that week he'd agreed with someone on that.

"He was a good man."

137

Tom hesitated, but then said: "There's no hell like losin the one you live for."

"I stewed these last few days, just thinking of this moment, trying to get up the nerve." He let out a long sigh. "I wanted retribution. I wanted to throw *you* into a fucking tree. But now I'm standing here crying like a little girl."

"Ain't no shame in that."

"Yeah, well..."

They stood there in silence for another moment as Andre tried to collect himself.

"Look," Tom said. "It won't be easy, but it'll be easier if you just accept that it was an accident. This here, this ain't gonna solve nothing. It'll just make things worse. I think you know that."

Andre waved his hand in a gesture of passivity. "Relax, Hargrave. I'm not gonna kill ya. Even when I came in here I knew that. I really just wanted to scare ya, maybe rough you up a little bit."

"Well, you certainly did all that."

"I guess I did."

"If you can forgive me, I can forgive you. We're grown men. What happened here tonight can stay between us."

Andre moved forward slowly, his hand outstretched, open. Tom shook it.

"I'm sorry," Andre said.

"Me too."

The big man looked him in the eyes. "I'm a detective. I can tell when people are lying, and you're not. You really didn't have a motive, and you don't strike me as a killer. I know what happened with Mrs. MacDougall, but the woman was unhinged. Anybody would have done the same. I think you and Marty had an argument that escalated quickly, and maybe you threw a few punches, but I don't think you killed him."

"That's the God's truth."

Andre sighed and rolled his shoulders. "Well, I'll show myself out."

They moved together through the kitchen toward the doorway, Jep calm now and licking at the man's hand.

"I had a dog like this once, a long time ag—" Andre stopped talking suddenly, a guttural sound coming out of him as he curled forward.

Jep stepped back and Tom turned to Andre, watching as blood spat from between the man's lips. There was a wet sound, and then he groaned again, falling to his knees, revealing Paige standing beside him in the shadows, a bloody knife in her hand.

Tom pulled her away from Andre before she could send the blade into his side again. He snatched the knife from her hand and went to the Andre's side. The big man's eyes were glazing as he held his stomach, blood seeping out between his fingers in hot, red rivers. From the placement of the wound, it looked like Paige may have hit organs.

"Jesus," Tom said, looking to Paige, then Andre, then back again.

"Call... 911," Andre said between coughing up blood.

Tom looked to the phone on the nightstand and was about to go to it, but something stopped him. This was yet another violent crime at the Hargrave residence. As he stared at Paige—at the sheer, bottomless blankness of the girl—he felt lost in a black pool of uncertainty.

"Please..." Andre gargled.

Tom stood up and moved toward the phone, his hands shaking.

If I call and the police come out here and see what Paige has done...

What would people think?

Where the hell did she get that knife from?

It was a butcher knife, but there was no way she could have snuck into the kitchen to grab one without them seeing her, as there was only one doorway.

Christ, if this gets out, everyone is going to believe what Fay and Sands have been saying about her, that there's a killer inside my little granddaughter.

Tom touched the phone, smearing it with blood. He still didn't lift the receiver.

"Help me!" Andre said, trying to shout but only managing a wet whisper.

Tom's fingers moved away from the phone.

CHAPTER THIRTY-ONE

"You were upstairs the whole time."

Paige still had a distant look in her eyes, two lost planets drifting further and further from the sun.

"Hey!" He shook her.

She glanced at him.

"You were upstairs," he said. "You didn't see anythin."

"Okay."

"I killed this man, Paige. Not you. He was an intruder, and I stabbed him."

He picked up the knife and turned it over in his hand, a butcher knife with a foot-long blade, unlike any he owned.

"Where did you get this?"

The girl looked away, and Tom knew.

He gulped. "This… this is the knife that killed Alice, isn't it?"

Paige turned to the side, looking further away from him, her chin tucked. Anger flooded Tom in a crushing tsunami, making his eyes bulge and veins throb in his neck.

"Answer me!"

He wanted to hit her so badly that his knuckles stretched taught and cracked from the pressure of his clenched fist. The bruising throbbed.

"Why do you have this, Paige? *Why?*"

"He was going to hurt you!" She pointed to Andre. "I had to stop him!"

"Honey—"

"Mrs. MacDougall was going to kill me, so you killed her!" she said, tearing up. "It's the same thing. I didn't wanna do it, but I had to save you!"

He felt his throat turn to burlap.

"I know, honey, I know, and it's okay. You did the right thing."

He didn't have the heart to tell her what had just happened between him and the man who now lay dead on the floor with a tablecloth draped over him. He didn't want her to have to live with that knowledge.

"If I did the right thing, then why do we have to lie?"

Tom didn't have an answer for that, at least not one he wanted to give her.

"It's just better this way," he said. "Trust me."

She stared at the floor. "Alright."

"But I need to know why you have this knife."

She fell silent again, guilt smeared across her face.

"Where did it come from, Paige?"

He scooted closer and touched her chin, turning her face toward him. They were mere inches apart, eyes locked, the coppery scent of blood all around them. Tom was afraid of what she might say, knowing that whatever answer she would give would be like a stabbing all of its own.

"The man in the woods," she said. "He dropped it."

There was something off about her body language—a slight tick in her face that he didn't like. She sounded like she was acting poorly in a school play she'd been forced into.

"You mean to tell me you picked up the murder weapon and didn't tell nobody about it, even after all that police questionin?"

Paige nodded, fidgeting.

"Why on earth would you do that?"

Now she shrugged.

"Paige! Do you realize how *terrible* that is? Jesus!"

He stood up, pacing back and forth, running his hand through his hair, feeling the sweat gathering in it.

Paige mumbled. "I didn't mean to."

"Didn't mean to? *Didn't mean to?* Paige, this is bad—very, very, awfully bad. This could get you in serious trouble. What the hell do you mean when you say you *didn't mean to*? You have it, dontcha? Here it goddamned is. How is havin it a goddamned accident?"

She didn't reply so Tom got down on his knees to look her dead in the face, but she kept dipping her head, staring at her bare feet, unable to meet his gaze.

"The police should've had this knife. You're a smart enough girl to know that. We have plenty of knives in this house. Why did you take this one?"

"I dunno."

"You must have had a reason."

Still nothing.

"Paige, we're in this together, understand? Fay, and this man here… we're in this *together*. But you have to be truthful with me. You have to tell me why you have this knife, and you have to tell me *now*."

The girl seemed to gather herself, straightening up and getting her chin high enough to look at him. Her eyes were dry now, her features slack.

"Because it looks like a sword," she said.

Tom was still. "What?"

"It's longer than most knives. It looks like a sword, like it came from Sopheria."

Tom put a hand over his mouth as his chest constricted. He shut his eyes tight.

"It's a sword, Grandpa," his granddaughter said. "The sword of the Black Lord Slagon."

～

Would they even want to inspect the knife?

He could say it was one of his own. It was old, but passable as a kitchen utensil. If he had used it in self-defense, why would they want to take it down to a lab? Even if they did, they wouldn't have any reason to try and match the blade with Alice MacDougall's stab wounds, would they?

Sure they would. After all that's happened here over the past few days?

He told himself that he was tired and not thinking straight, that he was just being paranoid. But Alice had been killed with a large butcher knife that they'd been unable to find in the woods, and now here one was, bloody and in the hand of the man who'd discovered Alice's body.

Maybe they're going to start looking into me now.

It made sense. After all, he'd found Alice, shot Fay, and now he'd stabbed Donati's partner. The latter would even raise further questions about Donati's little accident. Tom was surprised they hadn't come at him over that one as it was.

This could paint me as some kind of serial killer.

No, Tom, come on. These were self-defense killings. Justifiable homicides. And everyone knows you had nothing to do with poor Alice.

But the bodies just kept piling up. His ranch was becoming a slaughterhouse, only with human carcasses instead of steers. It was bound to make the police suspicious at this point, wasn't it?

What the hell am I gonna do with this knife?

He thought about the tire tracks he'd made in the road and how he'd used Donati's car to cover them.

You could stab him in the wound with a different knife, one of your own.

But it was just a passing thought. He couldn't bring himself to stab the man deep in his belly, even if he was dead already.

That left him with the same question.

So what do I do with this knife?

They could compare it to the records of Alice's wounds. Hell, they could even exhume Alice to compare the knife to the wounds. If they do, then how do I explain my ownership of it?

A new though hit Tom and he looked at the man on the floor. A chill went through him as a plan started forming, a black mushroom cloud of deception.

Andre brought it in with him.

But how would that work? This man had been brought into the mix *after* Alice's death. He was a private investigator, or at least an assistant to one, who'd been brought in to solve the case. Why would he have Alice's murder weapon?

No one's gonna think it is Alice's murder weapon. They'll just think he brought a butcher knife in with him. Right?

But why would he do that? He had a pistol on him.

It hadn't been fired.

Just hide the gun somewhere and bury it later.

But that still doesn't help with the big question they're all going to have: why did this man want to kill you, Tom?

The more he thought about it all, the more mixed up he got. It was a puzzle so scattered it was nearly impossible to tell if any pieces were missing.

I don't know. When they ask that, just tell them you don't know.

Another thought hit him and hit him hard.

Sands.

This man worked for Sands, right? And you just shot Sand's sister. So there's your answer.

A hit man.

Tom took a deep breath as the epiphany thundered through him.

Sands put a hit out on him, and paid the man to kill him. The guy was not just a detective, but also a hired gun. Donati had been a crooked cop, and Andre was in cahoots with him. It was easy enough to believe that he was dirty too, and Tom wondered if the guy had ever had any run-ins with the law. If he had, the story would stick even easier. Tom had already made it clear to Dale that he was worried about what Sands would do. In addition, he'd told Dale that Donati and Andre had approached Paige at school, and he had the Godfrey boy as a witness to it. Tom and Paige had been harassed. The barn had burned. Sands had gone after him legally, but it just wasn't enough to satisfy his thirst for vengeance. It all added up.

But it isn't true.

He knew that, of course.

But it's the clear way out. It all just falls together.

It could even explain the knife. Perhaps Sands chose it as an eye-for-an-eye sort of thing, in revenge for Alice. He'd sent the hit man in with a knife just like the one that had killed his niece, a death that had driven his sister to madness and ultimately resulted in her death at Tom's hand. It was symbolic.

But Sands will go to prison.

But he might not. He's a rich man and can afford good lawyers that will find loopholes and such to get him off.

But they might not.

He could still go to prison.

Well, Sands can go to prison, or you can go, and possibly Paige too.

Tom crossed his arms and caught his reflection in a picture frame. It was a picture of Dawn, sitting on a park bench in the fall, russet leaves all about, and little Paige sitting on her lap, smiling with her mother's arms wrapped around her. Superimposed over it now was Tom's face, glowing a somber blue in the light of the moon.

A promise is a promise.

CHAPTER THIRTY-TWO

Dale had to sit down.

Through the house his men worked. Cameras flashed. Tape stretched. Examinations were done and the scene was investigated like all the others. It had become a familiar routine, a strange ritual.

Tom and Dale sat in the kitchen.

"Sorry to drag ya out so late," Tom said.

"I had to be here, Tom. To see for myself."

"Whadda ya think?"

Tom had been careful not to lead Dale. He figured the story he'd come up with was one the sheriff would conclude on his own. The circumstances would call for nothing else.

"This man is Andre Trotter," Dale said. "He was Donati's assistant."

"I believe he's the same man who was snoopin around my barn before it burned down. Fred Hollister saw him. He might be able to identify him."

Dale nodded, a long breath escaping him. He seemed downtrodden, a man aging before Tom's very eyes. "I just don't believe it."

Tom's whole body tensed. "Believe what?"

"I know it's true. I'm seein it. But I just can't believe it. I'm shocked."

Tom's shoulders began to relax. "So what're ya thinkin?"

"Tom, this man worked for Sands."

"I know."

Tom held back, wondering if he could bring himself to say what he knew he needed to. Once the lie was told he would have to stick with it, no matter what. And if he told it…

"When this man attacked me," he said, "he told me: *This is for Fay.*"

Dale pulled back, crossing his arms. "I hate to admit it, but you were right about Sands. I just can't believe he'd do somethin this crazy. Sweet Jesus."

"So, you think he paid this man to kill me then?"

"Don't you?"

"Ayuh, but I wanted to hear you say it. You're the sheriff."

"There's just no other reason why Trotter would *want* to kill you," Dale said. "This seems loud and clear to me. I think Sands paid these two so-called *detectives* to stalk Paige and burn your barn. He wanted to get at you. But then, when Fay died, he snapped and upped the order to murder."

They were quiet for a moment, then Tom said: "What happens now?"

Dale's face was hard. "A warrant for Sand's arrest."

⤛

Dawn broke over the ranch, a sliver of pink light turning into a pallor blue that swallowed the land, dyeing it, making everything look tinted by steel. Official vehicles came and left, creating a spectacle that turned the heads of Tom's neighbors when they drove by the house on their way into town. He saw their shocked expressions and instantly knew he would never be looked at the same way again. How could Russ Redburn and Hannah Green ever just have a normal chat with him over piping-hot chicken and waffles? After all that had happened, how could he ever hope to repair his relationship with the butcher Jeff Summerson or Hannah's husband, Ed? His ranch was now the death ranch, a valley of murder and carnage. It would become a place kids dared each other to walk past. Teenagers would camp out in the woods behind it and tell ghost stories while they drank beer and smoked pot, the boys scaring the girls to get them to snuggle closer. It stood to reason that the townsfolk would be less and less interested in buying his meat. He would lose more partnerships and fail at auction. He knew these truths because he knew Middlebury. Rumors and scuttlebutt had tarnished many good people, and with less dirt than what folks had on him now.

Watching yet another body carried across his driveway, Tom felt not just tired but decrepit, beaten into the earth like a railroad spike. He had an ache in his bones that matched the one in his soul; a hopeless soreness he knew would stay with him. He would not be able to fix it with therapy or even drown it in booze if he fell off the wagon. It had burrowed deep. It would live inside of him until he was gone, resonating like the sound of a cello in an abandoned theater.

As he watched the police finish up from his living room window, a twinge snaked up his spine. His head grew fuzzy, almost dizzy, and he put his forehead against the glass. Guilt permeated him—for the blood that had been spilt, for the lies he let others believe, for all the terrible things he'd done.

But raising a child meant doing things you didn't want to do. It meant that you put everything you had into taking care of them in every possible way. You spent time, money and energy on someone other than yourself, twenty-four hours a day. It meant complete and utter devotion, excluding all others, even oneself.

Raising a child, Tom had finally learned, was all about sacrifice.

CHAPTER THIRTY-THREE

Two days passed.

The sun returned, melting a good deal of snow and leaving cold mud in its wake that froze overnight. The days were pleasant, and he let Paige sled up and down the slope that lead to the trail, but only when he was outside with her. Though he took no real joy in it, Tom tossed a tennis ball to Jep to give him exercise. The dog chased it but there wasn't as much of a skip in his step as there had once been. Tom knew just how Jep felt.

Paige seemed to be in good spirits, considering. She was still quiet and pensive, but she didn't seem stressed or frightened by the recent events. She didn't wake up from nightmares and come running into his room at night, and there were no tears from her like there should have been for a little girl who had just killed a man. Instead there was just her usual distance, as if her spirit had flown into some unseen netherworld long ago, leaving behind a body run by an automatic machine. She played, but by herself. She watched cartoons, but didn't laugh. She ate dinner, but mostly picked at it. And most of all she stayed in her room. Tom knew why. She was scribbling in her notebooks, continuing the saga of Sopheria, likely dragging the characters through fates even darker than the ones of her own reality.

Tom wouldn't take her to Dr. White anymore. He couldn't risk having the truth slip out. He was worried enough that she may somehow get them caught in their lie without inviting a shrink to poke and prod. He also didn't let her return to school, and he didn't go back to his ranch work. He let Willard Hollister handle the livestock and took a break from everything else. There was too much to sort out. He wasn't sleeping well and couldn't concentrate during the day. When he did sleep, he grinded his teeth so hard that he woke up with his jaw aching so badly he couldn't chew breakfast. His nerves were like burnt wire, smoldering inside of him, and the muscles in his neck ached from the constant tension. His stool was runny. He felt like he might be getting an ulcer.

Maybe I should see a shrink myself.

He busied himself around the house to take his mind off things— mopping, spraying WD-40 on door hinges and fixing wobbly table legs. He made big vats of chili to freeze and changed the oil on the truck. These tasks were simple enough for him to accomplish and helped connect him to normal life, which had been pulling away from him like an ebbing phantasm. Life was no longer something he could grasp. It was nebulous and unfamiliar, a distorted version of its former self. The old life he'd had that had given him grief and hardships and challenges—the life that had given him a wife and daughter only to take them away—seemed utopian compared to the black hell that held him now. Here there was fear, emptiness and despair. There was yellow guilt and frenetic paranoia, anxiety that diseased the body, shame that made him hide.

When all was silent, he could hear the gunshot that killed Fay and the blood-wet pleas of Andre. When Tom closed his eyes, he saw gushing wounds, a skull shattering like glass, and Donati's twisted head crushed against a tree, his arm bent behind it in a gruesome hood. And he could smell the rich scent of Alice MacDougall's blood, just as fresh as when he'd found her on that fateful afternoon.

What was it that Betty always said at tough times?

Oh, that's right: This too shall pass.

He wanted to believe Betty. He wanted to trust in her words and in his own strength. But doubt nagged him, snickering as it circled him, and grief came from all angles with the tenacity of ravenous wolves.

⤳

The morning that Dale came by the house, he arrived in his cruiser and in uniform, unannounced. Though it was past noon, Tom and Paige were both still in pajamas, her watching TV while he read the paper. He'd been scanning it every day, hoping for some sort of information about the Sands case now that the man had been arrested. The paper didn't offer much, and he hadn't heard anything from Dale and had been too scared to pry.

Seeing him pull up, Tom opened the front door, closing his robe tight against the wind. Dale came up the walk with his head low, looking at his boots as he moved. He didn't look up at Tom until he reached the porch, and when he did his face was stern.

"Mornin, Tom."

"Dale."

"I'd like to have a talk with ya."

His stomach dropped. "Sure thing, come on in."

Tom stepped aside, hoping his nervousness didn't show.

"No," Dale said, "I mean down at the station. I'd like you to come with me. Paige too."

Tom forgot to breathe. He could feel the blood leaving his face as a numbness rushed in. He forced himself to nod.

"Alright," he said. "Just let us get dressed."

"Of course."

Dale stepped inside and Tom led him into the living room. Paige looked up at them, her face like a statue's.

"Darlin... get dressed, we're goin down to the station, okay?"

"What for?"

"Just do like I tell ya."

She got up and clicked the remote to turn off the TV. The lack of the noisy cartoons gave the room an eerie calm that Tom's anxiety fed off of.

"Excuse us," Tom said to Dale.

The sheriff hovered near the spot where Tom had let Andre Trotter bleed to death after his granddaughter fatally stabbed him.

Once upstairs, Tom whispered to her. "Remember what we talked about. Just stick to the story, no matter what."

Paige nodded. "Okay, Grandpa."

Once they were dressed, they met Dale at the foot of the stairs. The company stirred Jep, so Tom shooed him away but tossed him one of the deer antlers he kept in a bucket on top of the hope chest.

"I'll follow ya?" Tom asked.

"Why don't you two just come in my cruiser."

"Well, alright then."

Tom tucked his hands into his coat in an effort to keep them from shaking. Dale's serious tone was worrisome, but not as much as his insistence that they all drive to the station together. There was something so final about that, as if they were never going to come back.

He knows the truth. I don't know how, but he knows what we did to Andre, and maybe what I did to Donati. He knows how we set up Sands. He knows about...

Then it hit him.

The knife.

They'd taken it, of course. Evidence. Tom's throat went dry, thinking the knife had given something away, had told a tale as big as all the valley.

Calm down. You don't know what all Dale knows. Play innocent until you do.

He knew he should wait until they got to the station, but he couldn't bear the suspense of the silence. If he was suspected, or worse yet buried by hard evidence, he would rather know now than sweat in the back of the cruiser all the way into town.

"So what's going on?" he asked. "Some break in the case?"

"Sort of. I'll explain when we get there."

Dale made a motion with his head toward Paige, indicating that he didn't want her to hear.

Or that she's *the break in the case*, Tom thought.

A young officer took Paige to the waiting area, letting her sit and play with some of the toys they kept in a bin. Dale escorted Tom to his office and when they walked in Tom saw that the same man who had interviewed Paige, sergeant Deontay Cole, was leaning against a file cabinet.

"Sergeant," Tom said.

"Mr. Hargrave."

Both men nodded but neither tried to shake the other's hand.

Dale motioned to a chair and Tom sat down, Dale sitting on the edge of his desk. Tension thrummed in Tom's temples. He wanted to devour his fingernails.

"Tom, the reason I brought you in here was to talk to you about Gerald Sands."

Tom cleared his throat. "Okay."

"As you know, we've arrested him for conspiracy to commit murder."

"Ayuh."

Tom was chewing on the sides of his tongue, resisting nerves that urged him to babble. Dale, however, seemed to struggle to find words of his own.

"Though he denies it, it seems that Sands hired Andre Trotter to kill you, out of revenge for his sister. He admits to hirin Trotter and Gagliardi—or Donati as he called himself—to look into you and Paige, but nothin more. It seems to make sense that he had these men torch your barn, and your neighbor Fred Hollister confirms that Trotter is the man he saw snoopin around it."

Tom stayed silent as he waited for more.

"The knife that you stabbed Trotter with…" Dale said, trailing off. "This knife is the one you say Trotter came in with. You say he was tryin to kill you with it, even though he had a gun on him?"

"Ayuh."

"That's right?"

"That's right."

"Well, this is where it gets really interestin."

Again, Tom waited, feeling doom closing in on him.

"You see, Tom. We ran forensics on the knife."

Tom remembered that he had wiped the handle clean of any of Paige's prints, put the knife in Andre's hand, and then back into his own.

"We ran the forensics," Dale said, "because we had a sneakin suspicion about it. See, the knife was the same type of knife we'd combed those woods for all that time. It was just the kind of blade that had caused the wounds on Alice's body. And, in fact, we discovered that it was the *exact* knife that had caused those wounds."

Tom felt nauseous but still tried to play along. He put shock on his face by opening his mouth and eyes wide.

"It was?" he asked. "It was the same knife?"

"The lab matched it up with Alice's wounds. There's no doubt that it was the same knife. And that brings us to a very big question: why did Andre Trotter have it?"

Tom sat there, unsure which way this was going. He gave off a small shrug and turned up his palms in a gesture of ignorance.

"We think we know," Dale said. "We think that Andre Trotter is the man that killed Alice MacDougall."

Of all the bad scenarios Tom was imagining, this had not been one of them. He couldn't help but go slack in the chair. A tidal wave of relief washed over him, cleansing him despite the confusion it brought. He felt safe. Better than that, he felt Paige was safe.

"Trotter? You think Trotter killed Alice?"

"We do. And what's more, we think Sands hired him to do it."

Tom's draw dropped, and not for show this time. "But... why?"

Dale moved from his desk. "Whenever a child is killed, the killer is almost always a family member or someone very close to the family. Just like we'd talked about before. People always think that lone nutcases do these killings, but that's just movies and sensationalistic news headlines. Random child murderers are rare."

"Most of the time," Cole added, "someone in the immediate family is the culprit. So when a kid is murdered, a very thorough investigation is done of the child's family. We turned over every stone here."

"That we did. Troy MacDougall was clean, as was Fay MacDougall. Nothin on them at all and their grief was true and awful. Only Uncle Gerald seemed to take things in stride. I first noticed it at the wake. He seemed so cold and unfeelin. Now, he's a business man so maybe he's learned to push down his emotions and keep composure, but…"

"You think Sands paid someone to kill his *niece*?"

Tom's head felt tight. He'd known he was setting Sands up for conspiracy to commit murder, but he'd never planned to link the man to Alice's death.

Dale went on. "When Alice died, the first thing Sands tried to do was pin it on someone. Now, it's normal for a man to want answers at a time like that, but Sands kept *pressin* when there was nothin to be found. He would've been happy to let Reston take the wrap, but when we cleared him Sands needed a new scapegoat. By that time, Fay had gone haywire and was insistin that Paige wasn't tellin the whole truth; so Sands went after Paige, and then he went after you, whether or not you had anything to do with Alice's murder."

"It's textbook," Cole said. "He was panicking. We think that maybe something in the plan was botched, either by Trotter or Sands or maybe even Donati, and Sands was rushing to cover his tracks, hoping to use you and your granddaughter as stool pigeons."

"You said it yourself, Tom," Dale reminded him. "Back when the barn burned. You said he protested too much."

"But why would Sands wanna kill Alice?"

"Well, that's the million-dollar question. Usually a family-on-family killin is about money, but Sands was the rich one in the family and he wasn't gonna collect on some sort of insurance after Alice's death or anythin like that. So that leaves a crime of passion."

Tom squinted. "Passion?"

"So to speak," Cole said, "meaning that Sands might have been jealous of his sister's relationship with her daughter. He's also seen as a very cold and emotionless man, and he has no family of his own, so he might have wanted an opportunity to show just how much he cared about his extended family. The funeral was a big deal, and he made sure everyone saw just how dedicated he was to his sister during her difficult time."

"Of course these are just speculations," Dale said. "But it could've been anythin, or a combination of motives. In fact, the main theory I hate to admit we're lookin into is that Sands might have had Alice killed to keep her quiet about somethin."

"Like what?"

"Well, like I said, I hate to bring it up, but Gerald Sands has a record as a sex offender. It was just one offense, of course, and it was back in the '90s when he was twenty. He had sex with a girl who was only fourteen and got busted for statutory rape. Now that was the only time, and he went on record sayin he had no idea she was that young, and his daddy's lawyers managed to get him off without time served, but that mark is still on his record."

"So, you're sayin he's a pedophile?"

"These are just speculations. We can't rule anythin out. If he molested Alice then he has a motive to have her killed, especially if he was worried she'd talk or even that he'd just keep on doin it. He might've had her killed to keep himself from rapin her."

Tom just sat there, taking it all in.

His lies had worked, perhaps a little too well. But something still felt off, as if this was all some elaborate trick to get him to confess.

They're trying to get me to slip up somehow, to crack under the guilt of framing Sands.

"The fact is we don't know *why* yet," Cole said. "But we have every reason to believe Sands is behind these strings of killings and attempted murders."

"Killings?" Tom asked. "As in, more than one?"

"Donati," Dale said. "We think Sands had him killed."

"*What?*"

"I know it's a lot to take in. Hell, when Cole and the boys started comin to me with all this shit, believe me, I nearly keeled over. But I need you to understand the scope of this thing before we can move forward."

Move forward with what? Tom wondered.

"What got Donati booted off of the force was numerous accusations of extortion. When he died, he had a briefcase in his car with a buncha folders in it. One of them contained information on you and Paige, which makes sense seein how he was investigatin ya. But there was another one with all sorts of information on his client, Sands. Didn't think much of it at first. But there's all sorts of business paperwork and contracts; stuff that doesn't prove Sands was up to anythin illegal or nothin, but could hurt Sands's business enterprises if they got out."

Cole nodded. "It seems that Sands invested money in American Farm Goods Division, which is Fresh Foods Corps's biggest competitor. There have been rumors of a buy out, but it's all hazy right now."

"I think Donati was blackmailin him," Dale said. "At first I thought that he was blackmailin Sands and maybe even Trotter over Alice's murder, and that Sands had paid Trotter to off Donati. But, well, when we looked into that…"

Dale trailed off. Tom waited.

"They were lovers," Cole said. "Donati and Trotter."

Tom feigned surprise. "They're gay?"

"That's right, a couple of queers."

"They even lived together," Dale said. "Kept their love clandestine, but there's enough evidence in the apartment to prove they weren't just roommates, and we interviewed a few friends who confirmed they'd been a serious couple for the past few years."

"So then…?" Tom asked.

"We think Sands hired Trotter to kill Alice, and then Donati and Trotter to investigate you to pin the murder on Paige, the only witness. Then Donati tried to blackmail Sands, so Sands hired a third man to assassinate Donati, someone good too, because the killin really did look like an accident at first. But there's more to that than you know. We didn't release it to the press, but Donati had a gun on him that had recently been fired. We found shells at the scene. So we knew somethin fishy was up. In fact… and I hate to admit this too, but for a moment there we were lookin into *you* on that one."

Tom looked away. Dale went on.

"But that didn't add up any more than our idea that Fay had killed Alice, which entered our minds after seein how she went after Paige. We think Trotter maybe didn't know that Donati was blackmailin Sands, that he wasn't a part of it at all and didn't know Sands had killed his lover. He stayed on Sands's payroll, and when Sands decided to have you killed he put Trotter on the job."

Tom was glad he was sitting down.

Maybe they are serious. Maybe we're really off the hook.

"The reason I'm tellin you all this," Dale said, "is because there's one link in this chain we need to make this case stick. If we're gonna nail Sands' ass to the wall and keep it there, we're gonna need your help, Tom. We're gonna need you to help us get Paige to open up to us."

Tom nodded but said nothing.

"You've stated that Paige never saw Trotter the night he broke into your home," Cole said.

Tom purposely spoke slowly, so not to trip on his words. "That's right. She was upstairs when it all happened, and before she came down I put the tablecloth over him so she wouldn't have to see."

"That's why she didn't identify him," Dale said.

"Pardon?"

"That's why she didn't point him out as the man who killed Alice. I'm bettin if she gets a look at his face, she'll pick him out of the rest of those old mug shots."

"But—"

"I know, I know. Trotter doesn't match the description she gave at the time. She said the killer looked like Reston—blonde, tall. Trotter's muscly but of average height, and he's got dark hair and a dark complexion. But take a look at this."

He took a glossy off of his desk and slid it over to Tom. It was a picture of a man with platinum blonde hair and pale skin. He had to look closely at the face to realize it was Andre Trotter.

"See that?" Dale said. "Turns out Trotter used to be a hair stylist before he teamed up with Donati. He changed his look often by dyin his hair, usin tannin beds and even makeup. He's a real chameleon. We think he looked one way when he killed Alice, and then transformed himself into the tan, dark haired man he was when we tagged his toe. He deliberately changed his appearance to cover his tracks, see? So, if he was the guy in the car when Donati accosted Paige at school, she may not have recognized him then either." He pointed to the picture of the blonde Trotter. "We think that *this* is how he looked when Alice saw him in the woods, and that his muscular body made him just seem *big* to her, and she remembered that as *tall*."

"After all, every adult is tall to a child," Cole said.

The three of them fell silent. The intensity of the quiet was like cabin pressure. Tom found himself thinking of true crimes shows where people who had been wrongly convicted are exonerated after years and years in prison. He always wondered how it was possible for an innocent person to be convicted like that, how the police could screw it up and people could give false testimony to incriminate them.

Now he knew.

<hr />

I'm not a monster.

That's what Andre Trotter had said when Tom begged the man not to hurt his granddaughter.

I'm not a monster.

Now he was being painted into one, and Tom was being asked to pick up the brush.

As he sat there, Dale and Cole brought up Trotter's history as evidence of his low character. He had a few minor drug possession charges on his record but had assault charges against him from when a group of skinheads had crashed a gay bar and Trotter and his friends had kicked the shit out of them. These didn't seem like enough to paint the man into a killer for hire, but Dale and Cole leaned heavily on the man's personal history of what they called "sexual perversion". Trotter had been involved in all-male S&M clubs in his youth, and they were focusing on his relationships with other men who'd been arrested for lewd behavior and public indecency.

All they needed now was for Tom to point the final finger, or more accurately, for Paige to do it. The more complicated the mess became, the more lies Tom was roped into. He just hoped he could remember them all. Worse still was that Paige was now a part of these lies. Not only was this a poor moral lesson for her, it was also criminal behavior because she was giving false statements to the police. Down the road, she could be looking at perjury.

And then there's Sands.

While Tom didn't like Sands, he lamented the possibility that he may be sending an innocent man to prison for the rest of his life. Even if the son of a bitch had been responsible for the burning of his barn—and Tom couldn't say for sure that he was—it still didn't justify framing someone for murder. Tom had felt guilty enough by leading the police to believe Sands had hired a hit man. That alone would send him to prison, but now Sands was being molded into a child killer.

Trotter was already dead. His reputation might be tarnished but he wouldn't be seeing any jail time. But of course, that was Tom's fault too. The cover up had been cold and calculated. But he'd made his choice. He'd chosen to keep his promise, to honor his blood. He was going to protect Paige, no matter the cost, and no matter what fears peppered his mind.

The things we do for family.

So Tom agreed to help the police. He didn't see any other way around it. Sure, he could walk away from the whole mess and tell them he just didn't want Paige to have to go through all of this again, but that could lead to a court order, not to mention hostility and suspicion.

There was a clear problem with cooperating though.

Paige.

What would she do?

It was a question he could not answer. The girl was more than mysterious—she was nebulous. Tom never knew how she was going to react to things. She was a moody girl, with private thoughts and intricate, inner worlds. He wasn't sure just how well she would interview, even if he was able to tell her what the plan was. She would be interviewed about the incident in the woods all over again, and she would have to keep her story consistent with the one she'd told before. Worse still, down the road she would have to be able to tell the story in court, and hope that Sands' attorney couldn't poke holes in it and break her down like a dog shaking the life out of a rabbit.

They won't allow some lawyer to badger a little girl on the stand, he told himself.

But Paige still needed to keep her story straight.

If she identified Trotter as the man who killed Alice, then Dale had a clear case. If not, it threw a wrench in the works and would make things difficult for everyone, including Tom and Paige.

But Dale knows what he wants to hear. He's gonna hear it either way.

It was very possible that they would lead her more than they had before. Now that they had a clear suspect, they were all the more likely to feed her answers and make it very easy for her to finger Trotter, thereby catapulting Sands into a prison cell. They might be straightforward with her or they might go the cozy route and bring in Dr. White and Emma Rowe, the child-friendly officer who had interviewed Paige before. Tom suspected that no matter how the dance was done, it would end with the curtain falling on Sands.

CHAPTER THIRTY-FOUR

Tom never got a chance to talk to Paige alone.

They led him to the interview room and he and Dale stayed in there together while Cole went to get Paige. The room was stuffy and reeked of stale cigarette smoke. A water dispenser burped in the corner. Sitting in the hard chair, looking at the drab, tan walls, Tom felt broken and deeply insecure. Part of it was fear, but there was a greater instigator behind that fear: a harrowing, raw emotion he could not place. It was not exactly sadness or grief. It was the feeling that he was lost inside his own skin and no longer knew who he was. He felt as if he were watching what was happening from the outside, like he was seeing a play while also being an actor in it.

Across from him, Dale was a gray hull, audibly breathing through his nose, his hands crossed in front of him. The florescent lights made UFOs of the lenses of his glasses.

They didn't speak. They'd already said all that needed to be said.

The door opened and Paige walked in gingerly, followed by Cole. The door hissed closed and he brought her around the table toward Tom. She did not take her eyes off her grandfather as she approached, and when she sat down next to him Tom took her hand in his. Cole sat on the other side with Dale, both men smiling but somehow looking awkward for it.

"Okay, Paige," Dale said. "I know Sergeant Cole filled you in. You probably want to get back home and out of this borin place. Maybe set up your Christmas tree. But don't worry; this won't take long. We just wanna show you some pictures."

She was expressionless, saying nothing.

The two men looked to Tom for help, so he leaned in close to her.

"It's all right, darlin," he said. "Just some pictures. Nothin to be worried about." He hoped his words carried the reassurance she needed, that he was letting her know that she wasn't in any trouble. *We're okay*, he tried to convey, *they're not on to us.* "You just take a look at em. Then we'll go get us some candy down at the drug store. Twix Bars for you and Swedish Fish for me." He cracked a smile as an added bonus.

"Okay," she said.

Dale smiled at her. "Good."

"We're going to show you four photographs," Cole said. "We think that one of them might be the man who attacked your friend, Alice. You don't have to pick one out if you don't think it's any of them. Only pick one if it's the right man, okay?"

"Alright."

Cole brought the pictures out of a manila folder and lined them up in front of her. Each was in color—close, clear shots of the faces of different men. All of them had blonde or sandy hair and looked to be no younger than twenty-five and no older than forty.

The first picture, going from left to right, was of Reston, which struck Tom as odd seeing how he had already been cleared. However, the child had already pinpointed him once, so perhaps they threw him into the mix to see if she would revert to that choice. The next photo was a mug shot of a grisly looking man Tom did not know. The third photo was the same shot of the blonde-haired Andre Trotter he'd seen earlier, and the fourth was another mystery man.

Tom could feel his pulse speeding up. His throat closed and there was a stabbing at his temples. The policemen kept their eyes on Paige, who sat there with her chin down, examining the pictures without touching them.

Her hand remained in Tom's.

It began to move.

It didn't take Tom long to realize what she was doing.

The hand game.

She gave him three pumps and then one finger went into his palm.

Three. Yes.

He was so nervous that he didn't understand what she meant at first. She gave him the same code again, and then it dawned on him. She wasn't making a statement; she was asking him a question.

Number three? Yes?

She'd figured it out. Somehow she knew they wanted her to pick Trotter, even without knowing why. *Maybe it's because he was the new addition to the lineup*, Tom thought. *Or maybe it's because of what happened with him the other night.* Either way, the girl was sharp. She knew exactly what was happening.

Their hands were beneath the table where the policemen couldn't see, but Tom didn't think it made much difference. The movements were soft and subtle and only the two of them knew the codes. He looked at the picture of Trotter, into the dead man's sorrowful eyes, and gave Paige one finger in return.

Yes.

Paige leaned in closer, pretending to really examine the shots. Then she gasped and pulled away from them, hitting the back of her chair. Her face went slack with fear and her hand shook, putting on a real show as she reached out and pointed at Trotter's picture.

"Him," she said. "That's him! That's the man who killed my best friend."

CHAPTER THIRTY-FIVE

The moon was out early, slowly dragging the magic light of dusk with it. The valley whipped past the windows in a blur of desolation, and flurries fell like tears, few and far between. Dale had Deputy Struve drive Tom and Paige home after Tom had made good on his promise of stopping at the drugstore. They were in the backseat together, and the gummy candy gave his jaw something to do to release some of the stress that boiled inside of him like a kettle and whistled in his skull just as loudly. Beside him, Paige was savoring her last Twix, chewing off the caramel before going after the cookie part.

They'd been at the station longer than he'd realized. Both of them should be hungry, but Tom was too nerved-out and Paige was such a light eater anyway, so he told himself they didn't need to ask Struve to drop them off anywhere, that they could wait until they got home. But that wasn't the real reason he didn't take her to the Blue Streak Diner or even stop for a deli sandwich for the road and then catch a cab home. He really just wanted to shield both of them from the public eye.

From what Dale had told him, Fay's funeral was gearing up to be nearly as big of an event as Alice's was, and with the news of Sands being in the cooler, this made for a rather sordid story, one that was rocking Middlebury and dancing on everyone's tongues. Once word got out that Sands was also being charged with the murder of his niece, the town was likely to lose its collective mind. Tom didn't doubt it one bit. Small towns had a way of making the misfortunes of their residents into their own private movies, and this was easily the biggest movie they'd ever gotten. Tom wished he and Paige weren't two of the stars.

Paige ate her candy bar in silence and stared out the window at the rising moon and setting sun that fought for her admiration. Tom stayed quiet too, just wanting to get home to enjoy the illusion of safety that its walls offered.

When they got there, they hung their coats and kicked off their wet boots. Paige did not speak about the hand game they'd played at the station, nor did she talk about Andre Trotter. She didn't even ask why she was supposed to pick him as Alice's killer. She didn't ask about dinner. She didn't ask to watch TV or to play outside before it got full dark. Paige just excused herself to her room, and Tom watched her walk right over the spot where Andre Trotter had died, jump up the stairs, and take the steps two at a time. He'd grown sick of the sweet taste of the candy so he threw the rest of it in the trash with more force than was necessary. He sat down in his chair, knowing it all would catch up with him the moment he was alone. It had to come sometime, so he did not fight it.

He took his handkerchief from his pocket.

My God...

The ringing phone made him jump and he hollered. His heart raged against his ribs. Tom let it ring a few times, fresh sweat boiling in his hair.

It's Dale. Something's up. He smelled foul and somehow knew that it was all a bunch of filthy lies. He's trapped us and now he has us cornered with thirty officers outside, moving in on the house.

He picked up the phone slowly, almost hoping he was right because then it would all be over at last, over before the stress could put him on a hospital table with hoses up his nose.

"Hello?" His voice was cracking.

"Tom?" Mary asked. "Is that you?"

He sighed, having escaped prison once again.

"Ayuh, Mary, it's me."

"Are you all right? You sound, I dunno, drained."

"Rode hard and put away wet."

He wondered if she knew about the recent events, if word had traveled her way somehow. The last time they'd spoken he was telling her that he was afraid of the trouble he felt had been coming. Did she know just how big that trouble had been upon arrival?

"Have things gotten any better?" she asked.

That answered his question. She didn't know, and he wasn't about to tell her. He didn't have it in him to tell any more lies, even if they were the same ones being told to new people.

"Things are about the same," he said. "Just feelin run down is all."

"Yes, well, that's kind of why I'm calling. I was thinking about things and, well, I just feel like I should be doing more to help out. I mean, David hasn't been feeling good, but he's mobile, and heck, we're retired. So I was thinking that maybe we could come out there for a few days and lend you a hand."

He didn't respond at first.

"I was just thinking," Mary said, "you and that child have been through so much, and you are family. Besides that, I felt like Betty was looking down and wasn't too happy with her sister. I felt like I was disappointing her."

"Now, Mary, that ain't so. Betty loved you, don't go kickin yourself."

"I know she loved me, and I know she still does. I just don't want to fail her, or her grandchild, or you for that matter."

Any other time this warmth would have touched him, but now her words fell as flat as a greeting card, and her generous proposal left him feeling anxious, afraid. He wanted to hide from her, from the world.

"That's okay," he said. "You and David can just stay put. Things are turnin around here, really."

"But, you were just saying how you felt rode hard and—"

"It's been a long day is all."

"Well, that's what we want to help you with. We can watch Paige for you and help around the house so you have more time to take care of the ranch and make new partners."

"No, no, really, we're okay… besides, I'm thinkin about packin it in. Think I might be retirin."

"Really?"

"I ain't gettin younger. Maybe it's time I sold this ol' ranch. A man can't play cowboy forever."

"Sell the ranch? But that was you and Betty's dream."

"Yeah, well…"

He trailed off, lost and too exhausted to find himself or even a pale front as a substitute.

Dusk was settling in. The living room had grown dark without him noticing. The goose-necked reading lamp was on the end table beside him. He didn't turn it on.

"Oh, Tom. What is it? What's really eating you?"

I ain't being eaten at. I'm being quartered and flayed alive.

He looked out the window at the dark blue that was creeping over the valley, its shadows wrapping around the thicket like the fingers of giants. The snow was lavender and the fields were picked clean as an animal carcass on the side of the road. The flurries were steadier now, frenzied, and Tom sensed that even more snow was coming behind it, heavy and merciless, a blizzard to match the one inside of him. In the depths of his mind, he saw the snowy knoll of the clearing in the woods and recalled how a little girl's blood had turned it the color of smeared strawberries. He saw the wounds, deep into the stomach, just as they had been in Andre Trotter's side, and made by the same knife, a knife that Paige said belonged to a mysterious murderer she no longer seemed concerned about, if she had ever been at all.

"Mary?"

"Yes."

"You believe in souls?"

The question clearly took her off guard. "Souls? You mean, like, human souls?"

"Yeah. Like the soul inside a person."

She took a minute. "Yes, I guess I do, so to speak."

He was suddenly reminded of his conversation with Fay, the one about angels.

"Do you?" Mary asked.

"You know, had you asked me that a month ago, I think I woulda said no. But I've been thinkin about things differently lately."

"Since Betty died?"

"Betty…" he said, his wife's name falling from his mouth like ash. "Betty. You know somethin, Mary? After she died, I had this house to myself for the very first time, and it was the first time I'd ever lived alone in my entire life. Ain't that somethin? But this house… it has ghosts. Not just of the people who've died, but the people who just ain't livin under its roof anymore.

"I'd be in the livin room, and I'd hear footfalls upstairs. I'd go up, but there'd be nobody there. Or I'd be in the kitchen, makin supper, and I'd hear Scott and Dawn playin in the next room, like it was 1984. Sometimes, in my bed at night, I would feel the heat of someone lyin next to me, and I swear I could hear the little clickin noise that Betty made in the back of her throat when she was asleep.

"I don't know if that's my family's souls or not. I suppose most folks would say that they're just impressions on my mind, memories playin tricks on a lonely old man's head. But they felt like somethin more than that to me. Sometimes it spooked me. Other times I thought I was goin off my rocker.

"When Paige came to live with me, I thought it would be good to have life back in the house other than Jep and me. Little girls can bring a lot of light with em wherever they go, and I hoped she'd light up this old house like a summer day." He took a deep breath. "But you know somethin? It's only gotten darker."

"Oh my," Mary said. "It's just been hard for you both. There've been so many misfortunes."

"So you believe in souls, huh?"

"I do."

"Well then, let me ask you this. It's a question I've been havin trouble answerin. Maybe you can help me."

"Alright then."

"If there's such a thing as a soul, then can there be an absence of one?"

There was silence on the line.

"How do you mean?" she asked.

"Well, most people are born with two hands and two feet, right? But, now and then, some people are deformed and they ain't got no hands or feet. If people can be born without body parts, then maybe they can be born without *inner* parts. And I don't mean guts. Maybe people can be born *without a soul*."

"Oh, Tommy. I don't like that."

"But do you think it could be?"

"No, no. Everyone has a soul."

"Haven't you ever met someone that just seemed to have no life in em? Like the lights were on but nobody was home?"

"Well, I suppose."

"Everybody's met somebody like that, right? There are these people who just don't seem to feel anythin at all."

"Some people are just shy, introverted."

"I ain't talkin about no goddamned shy. I'm talkin about people who ain't got no heart. People who just don't *feel*."

"Well, people like that might be sociopaths or something. But I don't think that means they have no soul."

"What's a sociopath? That like a psychopath?"

"Sort of. It's a person who doesn't feel anything for others. No sense of empathy or pity. A person with no conscience."

"Christ, Mary… that's it. No conscience. No goddamned *conscience*!"

"Tom, are you all right? What's all this about?"

"Maybe there's not a complete lack of a soul, Mary, but there sure as hell must be soul damage. I'd say that's what havin no conscience is all about."

"You're not making sense."

"Don't I know it? Hell, none of this makes sense. How can someone be like that? How could someone just be *born* that way? It's just not right. Not right at all."

"You don't sound good. I really think we should come visit. I want to see you. I want to see Paige. It's been so long, it'd be like meeting her for the first time."

He muttered. "Looks like there's not much to meet."

"What?"

"Nothin."

He couldn't have them there. He couldn't have any visitors.

"There's no shame in needing help," Mary said. "Helping each other is what family is for."

Outside, the approaching night brought large, fluffy snowflakes that threatened to devour the world.

"Mary, you're preachin to the choir."

After convincing Mary to stay put, assuring her he was just tired and babbling about nothing, he hung up the phone and shuffled up the staircase, leaning on the banister in a crippled hunch. Exhaustion kicked at him like a horse that had just been branded, and his dark thoughts seemed to pull his body down, making his feet sink through each stair.

He did not eat dinner or ask Paige if she wanted any. He did not brush his teeth or change into nightclothes. He passed the bathroom and then passed Paige's door, not saying goodnight. Then he went into his bedroom and before he turned off the light he locked the door behind him for the very first time since he'd lived there.

CHAPTER THIRTY-SIX

Atop Essie, Tom wandered through the lonesome trails. The snow had been heavy the previous night and his drive to Hollister's place had been a difficult one, but he'd gone early and was able to avoid having to talk with them. He knew what they would want to talk about, and he just had no heart for it. He would have to chat with them when he came back with the horse and got his truck, but he would deal with that when the time came. Willard was taking good care of the herd, but Tom checked on them anyway and then took Essie out and left the note on the outside of her stall.

Betty would always take long, hot baths when she had something weighing on her, but Tom always took to horseback, no matter what the weather was like. Today the weather fitted his mood perfectly. It was below forty degrees and the air held dampness that hinted at more snow to come. The light, like the sky, was pale white, the world a fading tombstone of itself. Tom felt just as faded, just as bleak, for piece by piece he'd lost himself. His friends and sense of community had flown. The ranch now certain to close down. But more than that, he'd lost a clear sense of just who he'd come to think he was. He felt that he'd lost his grip on morality, that he had sacrificed his very soul to keep a sacred promise to his kin, the very kin he had once let down and was trying to make things up to.

Essie seemed happy to be with him and Tom wondered if Willard was giving her enough exercise. No matter where Tom might move, he knew he would have to have a barn for Essie. He could face giving up his cattle, though he did not know how he would pay his bills, but he could not part with his horse. Owning a horse was like owning a dog. Tom loved them like family, and he always had one. New horses and dogs never replaced the old, but they did continue a friendship between man and beast, a relationship that could not be paralleled.

Together he and Essie broke the snow as they journeyed the trails that wound through the woods like dead creeks. Mist burst from their nostrils, their breath the only sound in the hollow. The woods were theirs entirely, save for the occasional scurry of an unseen varmint or the flutter of passing wings.

When they got closer to the clearing Tom noticed the yellow police tape hanging from the trees. It had lost its tension and now lay half-buried in the snow and mud. They moved on, drawing closer to the thicket that surrounded the circle. Reaching the bushes, Tom could see over them and into the grove where his granddaughter was. She was standing in the center of the clearing with her back to him, but turned at the sound of the horse's hooves. She stared at him with eyes the color of a midnight sky. Her wool cap was on but her face was pink from the cold. It was the only thing that made her look alive.

"Hi," she said.

He nodded to her and dismounted.

She was standing in the exact spot where Alice had died. Snow had covered it, but the child had found it anyway. Tom suddenly realized that he was approaching her rather slowly. She held one of her bejeweled notebooks in her hand.

"Paige, what're you doin out here?"

"Nothing. Just playing."

"Playin where Alice died?"

She shrugged and looked around the thicket. "This is our spot. This is Sopheria."

There was an earnest longing to her that perplexed him. He stared at her until she looked away and sighed down at the snow at their feet.

"It was because of what happened there, wasn't it?" he asked.

"Happened where?"

"In Sopheria. The blonde princess and the Black Lord." He whispered hoarsely, the words coming out like smoke. "You said Alice was afraid of what he was gonna do. Did you disagree on what was gonna happen, or did the story become too real?"

She didn't respond.

"Was it the dark forces that caused it, Paige? Was it Slagon?"

Still he received no reply. She looked off into the distance, squinting as if there were something she was struggling to see, something beyond this world. He stepped into her and put his hand on her shoulder. His words fell even more hushed.

"Tell me the truth."

Tom's stomach went hollow, his limbs weakening with each breath. He tugged slightly on her shoulder and Paige came around to face him, looking so helpless, so innocent, and yet there was an underlined darkness to her, something brooding beneath the skin. He took her hand, removed her glove and then one of his own. He put her fragile hand into his, feeling the cool flesh of her small fingers.

"There was never any man, was there?" he asked.

Her face never changed. She did not admit anything, but she also made no effort to deny it. She held his gaze until he looked down and away, and then she turned back to the barren nothing of the snowy thicket. He waited for a pump of his hand, a signal in their private language, but she offered none. Tom looked up, seeing the dead tree limbs that covered the slate of the sky like claws. He felt that deep sense of loneliness again and realized there could never be a cap to it. Even the truth could not fill this fresh hole. He stood beside the child who had been left in his care, and together they stared at the clearing, swimming in its icy memories until Tom felt like he could drown.

"I want to go home," his granddaughter said.

Hand in hand, they walked through the brush to Essie. Tom leaned down, locking his hands to give her a boost into the saddle. Before she planted a foot in them their eyes locked. He was crouched down now and they were face-to-face, staring deep. He tried to find something in there, anything at all.

Once she was in the saddle he climbed up and sat behind her, feeling her tiny body against his abdomen, nestled there. He clucked and Essie began to carry them out of the clearing and onto the trail that lead to the comfort and safety of home. Snow flurries blurred the woods like static and the soaked sugar maples slouched over in mourning. In front of him, Paige was still and silent, a pond frozen over.

He put one hand on her shoulder, and then moved it further and slid his arm around in front of her protectively, hugging her close, shielding her as he always would, the way he'd been entrusted to by all the women he loved who'd come before her.

There was only one question left, but it was a question that no longer made a difference to him, a question that went on and on, and could lead only to an answer that had been there from the very beginning.

ACKNOWLEDGEMENTS

Thanks to Marc Ciccarone, Joe Spagnola, Andrea Dawn, and the whole team of misfits at Blood Bound Books. Thanks also to my good friends Gregg Kirby, Josh Doherty, Nicole Amburgey, my sister Danielle, brother-in-law John, and sweet, little niece Riel. I'd also like to extend tremendous appreciations to all my readers around the globe.

Big thanks to Tom Mumme—always.

And special thanks to Tangie Silva for bringing magic into my life for the second time.

ABOUT THE AUTHOR

Kristopher Triana is the author of *The Ruin Season*, *Body Art*, *Growing Dark*, *Full Brutal*, *Shepherd of the Black Sheep* and *The Detained*. His work has appeared in several magazines and anthologies, including "Year's Best" collections, and has been published in multiple languages. He's drawn praise from Publisher's Weekly, Cemetery Dance, The Horror Fiction Review and The Ginger Nuts of Horror.

He lives in Connecticut.

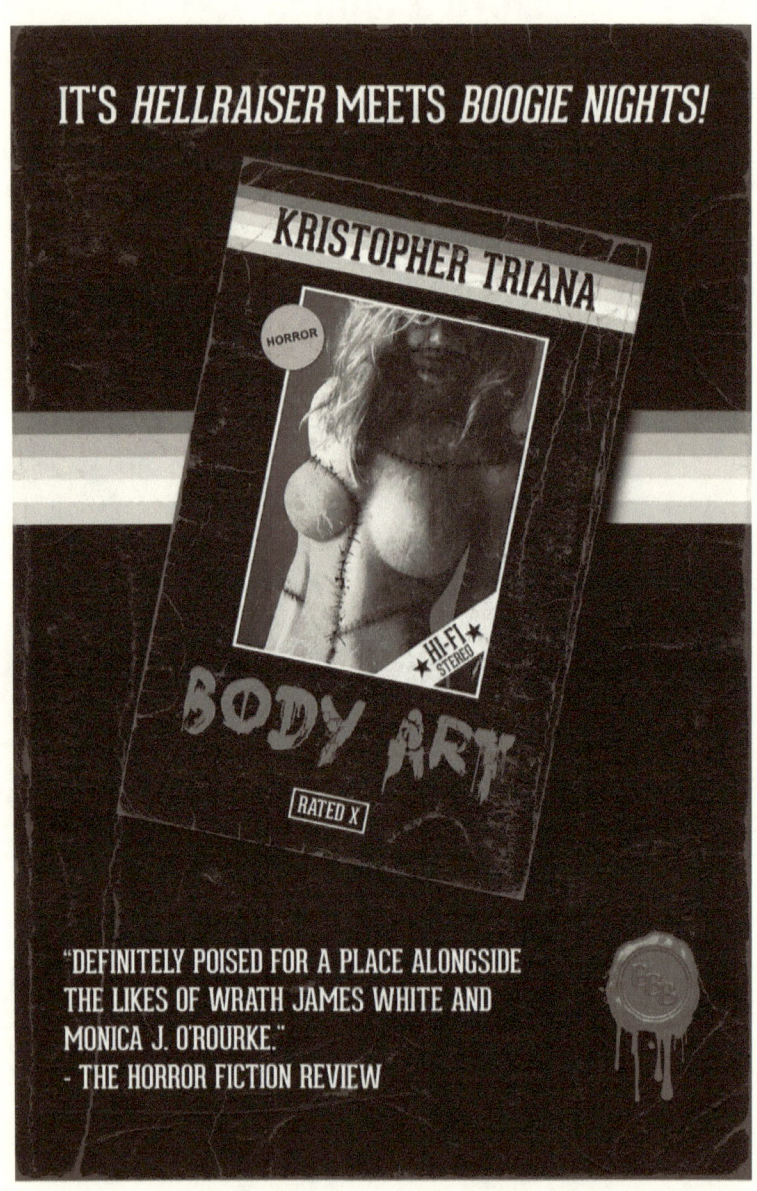

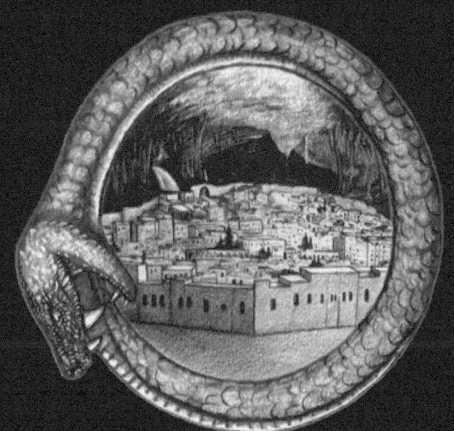